Ghosts Can Bleed

Ghosts Can Bleed

Tracie McBride

To my first-born child Declan, my first-born collection.

Acknowledgements

Thanks to all the talented people in the following writers' groups – Phoenix WSIG, Writers of Extraordinary Visions, SuperNOVA and Hopefull Monsters.

An extra-special thank you to the Dark Continents crew, for so many things, especially for taking the first chance on this manuscript, and to the Next Chapter crew for taking another one. Aroha nui, right back at ya.

Last Chance to See – *JAAM 2008, Top eight finalist for sixth Glass Woman Prize, reprint forthcoming in Devil Dolls and Duplicates in Oz Horror Fiction February 2011*, A Good Trade – *Staffs and Starships 2007*, Side Show Sally – *Abyss and Apex 2009*, Becoming – *Flash Me All Fantasy issue 2008*, The Last Tiger – *Electric Velocipede 2008, reprinted in Roar and Thunder 2010*, Nim of the Kamankay – *Lorelei Signal 2006, reprinted in A Time To… The Best of Lorelei Signal 2006*, Sun Stands Still – *Emerald Tales 2009*, Baptism – *Hecate 2009, Top ten finalist in seventh Glass Woman Prize*, House Arrest – *Antipodean SF 2007*, Killing A Goddess – *Coyote Wild 2008, reprinted in Writing Shift 2010*, Endangered Species – *Aoife's Kiss 2007*, After The Storm – *Barren Worlds anthology 2008*, One True Faith – *Short-Story.me 2009*, An Ill Wind – *Sybil's Garage 2009*, Trading Up – *Untied Shoelaces of the Mind 2010, The Way of the Buffalo podcast 2010*, Dreamcatcher – *Tales of the Talisman 2008*, Pierced – *Rose and Thorn 2007*, Lapp Dancing – *Pulp.Net 2006, winner of Spec the Halls contest 2008*, Fairy Gothic – *Andromeda Spaceways Inflight Magazine 2010*, Theft of A Servant – *Inclinations 2006*, Contact – *Kaleidotrope 2007, reprinted in Voyagers-A New Zealand Science Fiction Poetry Anthology 2009*, On The Border – *Sniplits 2008, reprint forthcoming in Fight On: Weird Enclaves and Black Pits anthology*, Ghosts Can Bleed – *Fictitious Force 2007, reprinted in Strangetastic 2010*, Portait of the Artist as a Young Mutant – *Aoife's Kiss 2007*, Rush Hour – *Big Pulp 2008, reprint forthcoming in Fight On: Weird Enclaves and Black Pits anthology*, Metal Mouth – *Nocturnal Ooze 2005, reprinted in DAIKAIJUZINE 2009*, Barking - *DAIKAIJUZINE 2006, reprint forthcoming in Dark Moon Digest 2010*, Offspring – *Space & Time 2009, Flesh Pot –AlienSkin 2005, reprinted in Aoife's Kiss 2008*, Whipping Boy – *This Mutant Life 2010*, Sleeping With the Fishes – *Win-*

ner of the Williamstown Literary Festival's Seagull Poetry Competition May 2009, Hit Single – *Everyday Weirdness 2010*, Fridge Wars – *Untied Shoelaces of the Mind 2010*, Tastes Like Chicken – *Illumen 2009*, Marked – *Edge of Propinquity 2007, reprinted in Shroud Abominations anthology 2008*, The Blue Screen of Death – *Flash Me 2006, reprinted in Between Kisses 2007 and WWW8 2009*, Hell is Other People – *Horror Garage April 2010*, Dark Wing – *Oddlands Magazine September 2008*, Waking Down – *Down in the Cellar June 2008*, Crimes of Faith – *Midnight Horror May 2007*, Diagnosis – *Alien Skin February 2007*

Contents

Last Chance To See

Early in 2007 one of my aunts announced that she had been diagnosed with terminal cancer. She had been given a few months to live (she went on to celebrate two more birthdays and a Christmas before finally succumbing to the disease). The family organised a mini-reunion to spend some time with her before she died. I drove with my three young children from one end of the North Island of New Zealand to the other to attend.

I was expecting a sad and solemn gathering, with lots of tears shed. Instead, we experienced macabre humour as my aunt described her experiences going shopping for the perfect nightgown to wear in her coffin, a moving yet strangely joyful moment when she distributed her few pieces of heirloom jewellery amongst her nieces, and hours of banality as the practicalities of feeding, entertaining and bedding down the multitudes were attended to. Even as we all contemplated death, the business of life carried on.

Afterwards, I got to thinking – what if everybody got to hold a pre-funeral? This is the story that resulted.

Sharon lifts her hand to her temple. She has a feeling that her head should hurt, but there is no pain, only the distant memory of it. Why should it hurt? She struggles to recall. She was driving home after a PTA meeting. There was another car, approaching too fast, too close, a sudden, tooth-rattling impact, and she was spinning, round and round and upside down and there was red, lots of red...

Her eyelids flutter open. Her husband Mark looks down at her. His eyes are bloodshot, and he looks like he has slept in his clothes. There is something wrong with her own eyes; her vision is slightly blurred around the edges, and she rubs at her eyes in a futile attempt to clear them.

"Sharon, Sharon," he says, "Can you hear me, Sharon?" He sounds like he is testing a microphone.

"Of course I can hear you," she says. Her voice sounds strange, as if it is a skilled impersonator who is speaking, using all the right Sharon-like intonations but lacking the exact configurations of her voice box. She tries to sit up, but her muscles don't respond as they should, and she can only raise her head from her pillow before slumping back down again. She looks from side to side.

"Where am I...what happened?"

Mark opens his mouth to speak, but a woman steps into her field of vision and silences him.

"I'm Dr Hayley Phillips," she says. "You were in a car accident. You died, Sharon. This is a reincarnation facility." Sharon looks to Mark, who nods confirmation, his throat working with barely contained grief.

"The avatar you have been transferred into has near-normal speech, hearing and vision and limited tactile sensation," Dr Phillips continues. "You are unable to eat or drink, so no Last Suppers, I'm afraid, and you are not equipped for...ahem...marital relations. Otherwise, you will function just as you did before death. Your avatar will hold your personality and memories for twenty-four hours. I suggest you spend a few minutes familiarizing yourself with it before joining your family."

Sharon shakes her head. "I don't understand...I can't take in any of this."

Dr Phillips bows her head. "I apologize if I seem a little brusque. It's just that most of our clients prefer to spend their remaining time on Earth with their loved ones, rather than conversing with me." She gives a wry smile, and Sharon starts to feel sorry for her before remembering that she is the one who is dead and in need of sympathy.

"Your husband has been fully briefed," Dr Phillips continues, "so he should be able to answer most of your questions. Otherwise, we have an after-hours information service." She slips a card into Mark's hand and leaves the room.

Sharon tries again to sit. Mark helps her, slipping a hand under her elbow and levering her into an upright position. She now understands what the doctor meant by 'limited tactile sensation'; it feels like Mark is touching her through several layers of gauze. Tears prick her eyes, or at least it feels like it, but when she tries to wipe them away, her hand is dry. The back of her hand looks unnatural. The skin tone is all wrong, it is too uniform, and there are no lines or visible veins.

What does the rest of me look like, she wonders. Her stomach knots with a sensation-that-is-not, a feeling that is already becoming familiar. She slips off the bed and stands swaying for a moment before shuffling to the far wall to stand in front of a full length mirror.

The knot in her stomach liquefies into nausea. "What have they done?" she whispers. The image that looks back at her is that of a life-sized Barbie doll wearing her face. Her borrowed body is more slender than her real one, with a sculpted waist and high breasts. She has no nipples, no pubic hair and no genitalia. The facial features are similar to her own, but minus the flaws, the acne scars and the laughter lines. She tries to smile and to frown, and the face in the mirror responds sluggishly. Had to wait until I was dead to get the body I always wanted, she thinks, and an involuntary giggle escapes her.

"Apparently, most people prefer to see an idealized version of themselves for their reincarnation," says Mark. "Anyway, your real body was too damaged to be able to take an accurate casting, so they recreated your face from photos and used Template B for the rest."

"The kids are going to be terrified when they see me like this," she says. "I feel like Frankenstein's bride."

"It's only for a day," says Mark. "They'll cope." He passes her an overnight bag. "I brought some of your clothes to change into. They probably won't fit properly, but it'll help you look more like you." Sharon dresses, looks in the mirror again, and grimaces.

"How are you going to pay for this?" she says.

"I took out a Terminal Extension on our insurance policies," he says, looking inordinately pleased with himself. He looks at his watch. "We'd better get moving. The police want to speak to you, you have to sign off on your will, and we have an appointment with the funeral director – and there are a lot of people waiting to see you at home."

* * *

The journey home seems too banal for Sharon's final hours of consciousness – same dented station wagon with sticky chocolate wrappers and children's odd socks hiding under the seats, same shabby suburban streets, same husband with the expanding bald spot and that annoying habit of swallowing loudly and frequently when under stress. At least he let me change the radio station, she thinks as she turns the volume up to drown out his gulping noise. She winds down the window, the early winter chill barely registering on her skin, and closes her eyes so she can picture herself cruising in a sports car with the top down along the coastline of a Mediterranean island with a Brad Pitt look-alike at the wheel.

Cars line both sides of the street outside Sharon's home, with more jostling for space on her front lawn. Her house is full of people, and there is a festive buzz in the air that stops cold when she enters the room. Her best friend Tania is in the kitchen, and she raises an eyebrow in casual greeting before returning her attention to the production line of food she is single-handedly preparing. She reminds Sharon of an elite Russian shot putter as she manoeuvres her 100 kilo frame through the confined space, simultaneously smoothing chocolate icing over a banana cake and warding off a swarm of sugar-starved children. Tania's father was reincarnated last year, Sharon remembers, which might explain why Sharon's appearance doesn't faze her.

"It looks like backstage on 'This Is Your Life' in here," she says, realizing too late how tasteless the joke is. Her mother and two of her aunts form a defensive huddle in one corner, drinks in one hand and hors d'oeuvres in the other. They put down their refreshments and start to wail when they see her, then they cut through the crowd in a wedge formation with her mother at the apex.

"My poor baby girl!" her mother says, stroking Sharon's plastic cheek. Sharon flinches; the last time her mother touched her face, Sharon was fourteen, and it had been a slap, not a caress. The sound of three sets of pounding little feet dispels the awkward moment.

"Mum's here! Mum's here!"

Sharon's children skid to a halt in front of her.

"Mum?" Her eight year old son Patrick looks from her to his father to her again. He reaches out a hand tentatively to touch hers, and then jerks it away. "That's not Mum," pronounces three year old Katie in her best adults-can-be-so-stupid-sometimes voice.

"Remember, kids," says Mark, "I told you Mum would look different. She's just borrowing this body for a day."

Five year old Gemma eyes Sharon speculatively. "A day?" she says. "Does she get her old body back after that?"

Mark shoots a pained glance at Sharon. "No, darling, after today she…"

"Oh, good," interrupts Gemma. "This one's much prettier." Her inspection complete, she runs off in search of more stimulating company. Katie takes one more look at the impostor posing as her mother and then follows her sister. Patrick stays, and he edges closer to her until she is able to embrace him. She buries her face in his hair. The body she inhabits cannot smell, yet still she imagines she is breathing in apple-scented shampoo. He pulls away from her after a few moments and looks at her with a pained knowingness that is far beyond his years, and Sharon feels a wrench in the place where her heart used to be.

Mark gets her settled into a comfortable chair in the lounge, as if such courtesies still mattered. There are many people who seek an audience with her – aunts and uncles, cousins, friends, neighbours, a few distant acquaintances who are ghoulishly interested in seeing a reincarnated person and who no doubt will be at the funeral tomorrow for the free food. Her sister Lisa arrives, tousle-haired and flustered after driving in rush-hour from the airport. She greets Mark with a kiss and presses her body for half a second too long against his, then lights a cigarette and takes a place on the edge of the throng around Sharon.

"Bloody typical," she says, releasing a plume of smoke out the side of her mouth. "Still getting all the attention, even when she's dead. Does anyone have any idea what I had to go through to get here? I had to put the flight on my credit card, and now it's over the limit. And do you know my work didn't even believe me when I said my sister had died? If they try to dock my pay, I swear..."

Sharon feels a quasi-headache coming on and rubs at her synthetic forehead. Her brother-in-law Andy walks in the door and the headache intensifies. Sharon gives Mark The Look, the one that says keep-that-idiot-away-from-me, and Mark gives back a Look of his own, the one that says he's-my-brother-so-suck-it-up. Andy stands in front of her and studies her with a lecher's practiced eye.

"Cool body," he says to Mark. "Not exactly true to life, though, is it? Sharon's tits were never that perky."

"I'm dead, Andy, not deaf," Sharon says through gritted teeth.

Andy has a few Looks too, and this one is all raised eyebrows and innocence, a what-did-I-say? Look.

Tania announces that dinner is ready, and everybody heads for the makeshift buffet set up on the deck. The food looks delicious, and Sharon looks on with envy as her guests eat and drink. Her mind imprint tells her that she is hungry, and she even tries to take a bite of roast chicken when she thinks that no-one is looking, but it just falls in a flavourless chewed-up mess from her mouth. She has a sudden vision of herself as Cookie Monster, masticating wildly on a cookie with crumbs flying from a wide fabric maw, and ducks her head to hide the blush that would have formed had her face been real. She feels a tug at her sleeve. Andy is back.

"Hey, Shazza," he says. She winces – she hates being called 'Shazza'. "I've heard that re-animated bodies don't have...." He stares fixedly at her groin.

"Andy..." says Mark in a warning tone.

"That's right, Andy. They're not entirely anatomically correct," says Sharon.

"Oh. Bit of a waste of money, then, if you ask me."

Mark takes a step closer to Sharon. "Nobody asked you," he says. Sharon feels a surge of love for him, the first she has felt since her reincarnation, and, if she thinks about it, the first she has felt for many months.

"Wouldn't have been any fun for you, anyway, Shazza," Andy says consolingly. "They reckon that you don't get much sensation in those bodies." He brightens as a thought occurs to him. "Hey – can you feel this?"

He plunges a fork into Sharon's upper arm. She yelps in surprise and jumps backward, tensing in expectation of pain, but there is only a dull and distant throb. A pale sap-like fluid seeps from the puncture wounds. Sharon's children start at the sound of her yell, and Katie starts to cry. All conversation around them stops, and people stare. Mark steps between Sharon and Andy, although who he is trying to protect is unclear.

"Good one, dickhead," Mark says. "I'm going to lose my security deposit now." Any tender feelings Sharon might be having for her husband dissipate as he steers her away into the bathroom and does a hasty patch-up job on her oozing arm. They rejoin their guests to find them already flowing into the gaps left by their brief absence. Andy has cornered Lisa, or perhaps it is the other way around. Sharon spends several precious minutes watching the pair manoeuvre in a complicated dance of flirtations and faux pas. One of her children is fighting with one of Tania's children, and Tania wades through the crowd to separate them.

"The kids are getting tired," says Mark. "I could try putting them to bed, but..."

"No," says Sharon, "let them stay up a little longer." Her aggrieved offspring wriggles free from Tania and runs, sobbing, for the comfort of Sharon's embrace. She looks around at her friends and family and wonders who will best be able to give her children solace this time tomorrow.

The cars on Sharon's front lawn play a polite game of dodgems as local visitors leave and a new wave of relatives arrives from late flights. Someone turns on the TV, and a crowd gathers around it to watch a rugby game. The kids run around in ever-decreasing circles until they collapse wherever they can find a space. Sharon crawls under the dinner table and gathers up Katie, who is curled up in a foetal position, snoring gently through the sporadic cheers that break out whenever the home team scores a try. Her cousin Kathryn pulls out a pack of cards and invites her into a game of Gin Rummy. Mark and her mother begin work on the conundrum of sleeping arrangements for the out-of-town visitors. A communal howl of despair rises as the opposition team scores. A slurred female voice yells out, "aww, just get over it, guys, it's not like it's life or death." Another voice shushes her in a drunken stage whisper. The rugby game ends and so does the card game and everyone drifts off to home or to bed or to sleep where they sit.

Sharon's temporary body does not know fatigue. Only Mark keeps vigil with her. They sit hand-in-hand in a dimly lit corner of the lounge.

"One extra day isn't enough," says Sharon. "I'm not ready to die. There was so much I wanted to do. I was going to write a novel. I was going to visit the Greek Islands. I was going to go to my children's weddings. I was going to celebrate my fortieth birthday."

Mark yawns and squeezes her hand. "How many people lie on their death bed and think, 'yeah, I've done all I want to do, today is a good day to die'?" he says. "Be thankful for the extra time you do have. Love everyone. The rest is all just padding."

Again Sharon feels phantom tears falling. She looks at her husband, surprised at his insight, but his hand has gone limp in hers and his head is nodding on his chest. She sits alone and waits for her last dawn.

A Good Trade

What is it with me and religion? I had a predominantly secular upbringing, so I can't claim to a childhood traumatized by the church. My experiences as an adult with organised religion have been overwhelmingly positive—I worked for a time for a community of Catholic Franciscan friars, and it was indisputably the best job I ever had. I have the utmost respect for people who draw strength from their faith and who strive to follow the message of peace from their chosen version of the Deity. Yet religion-gone-horribly-wrong is a recurring theme in my work.

"Don't go, Malik. Stay with me. Please."

My sister-spouse Nadia clutches at my arm. Her fingers dig into my flesh, her strength out of all proportion to her frail frame. Her pale eyes are silvery with tears.

I sigh and sit on the edge of her bed. She leans into me. Her heart beats as fast as a sparrow's against my chest. I enfold her in my arms, barely touching her for fear of breaking the veins that thread perilously close to the surface of her skin.

"We've been through this before, sweetling," I murmur into her hair. "As much as I would love to, I can't be with you all the time. Nothing bad is going to happen. You have your attendants to take care of you." I glance over her shoulder at the three Virgins assigned to her. They flank Nadia's bed, standing with heads bowed and hands clasped demurely in front of them. The one closest to me, Suri, is a big-boned, shapely girl, fresh off the farm, her tanned skin glowing against her white robes. She raises her head and meets my eyes, and I know in that instant that her title of Virgin will soon be rendered purely ceremonial, if it hasn't been already.

The attendants move in a pack to restrain and soothe Nadia as I pull away from her. We have played out this scene many times. Usually I walk away with Nadia's anguished cries ringing in my ears, but today it is different. She offers no resistance to the Virgins, and utters but a few words that send chills down my spine.

"Good-bye, Malik. I will not see you again."

* * *

Nadia does not say exactly when her prophecy will be fulfilled, but then, she never does. *I will not see you again,* she said. My first, crazed, impulse is to thwart her prophecy by merely avoiding her company, but I cannot bear the thought of living out my remaining days hiding in cowardice from a frail and harmless woman. So I seek a glorious death, taking a small hunting party with horses, hawks and nets into the mountains in search of gryphons.

It is said that if a gryphon finds you captivating enough, it will not kill you, but will only take a little of your blood, and might even grant you a wish in return, and in one desperate corner of my mind I hope that a gryphon's blessing might be powerful enough to over-ride Nadia's prophecy. I tense my neck at every sudden sound, expecting at any moment to feel talons tearing into my flesh, but the day ends without so much as a glimpse of a gryphon.

I court death in the dockside taverns next, where I flaunt a heavy purse and a disrespectful tongue, but even the foreign sailors know better than to touch the brother-spouse of the Royal Seer. I stagger back to the palace alone and unmolested.

I enter Nadia's chamber. Suri stands in a solitary vigil over Nadia's still form. I take her in a brazen act of lust and defiance while Nadia sleeps like a corpse in a drug-induced stupor. I draw away from her only when the first rays of dawn touch our sweat-slicked bodies as we lie entangled at the foot of Nadia's bed.

* * *

I desired Nadia once, with an intensity that eclipsed any fleeting feelings I might now have for her handmaidens. But of course, I only wanted her when she was forbidden to me. She was so different then, poised on the brink of womanhood, all long sun-kissed limbs and laughter. Then her first blood came, and with it her ability to See.

I was with her when she made her first prophecy. We were playing hide-and-seek in the corn fields just outside the town boundary. Finding her was always easy; she could never quite contain her laughter, so I had only to look for the tremor of the ears of corn beneath which she crouched while she held her hands clamped over her mouth and shook with suppressed giggles. I landed on her with a roar and tickled her mercilessly while she wriggled and shrieked, and I stole quick, furtive gropes at her budding breasts. She shook herself free and stood, looking at my face but seeming to focus on a point somewhere just beyond the back of my skull.

"The fields are burning," she said. "They will starve."

She said this softly, with a benign half-smile on her face, yet I felt a terror course through me as if a gryphon had seized me and borne me away. I gaped at her for a few moments while she continued to look through me, then she shook herself, her eyes met mine, and she burst into laughter again as she ran off deeper into the fields, daring me to catch her if I could.

And that was all. There was no speaking in tongues, no dramatic seizure, no levitation, none of the signs one might expect would accompany the uttering of a genuine prophecy. I might have forgotten about it, had the fields not caught fire some weeks later, just before the harvest. Some love-struck peasant and his sweetheart had crept into the fields at night with a lantern, and in the throes of their passion had knocked it over. The flames spread quicker than they could run, and they found their charred corpses where they had succumbed, barely ten paces from the edge of the field. The city had other food stores, of course, but not enough to adequately feed the entire populace, and the palace took what little there was for the nobles and their servants.

The townspeople had already buried the weakest of our number, and in our house we were eking out the last weevil-ridden contents of our larder, when I remembered exactly what Nadia had said. *They will all starve.* Not WE *will all starve.* THEY. Did that mean that our family would somehow miraculously be spared? In my naivety and hunger-borne desperation, I consulted a priestess and told her of my sister's words.

The priestess did not have an answer for me. In fact, she seemed distracted, as if she had barely heard what I had said. She promised to make an intercession for me and sent me off with an impatient wave of her hand to return to my hovel and await a response from the gods. I was happy to go, for I felt an elusive sense of revulsion in her presence. *Wait,* she had repeated, her heavy brows pressing together like two amorous caterpillars. *And make sure your sister waits with you.* I agreed as I backed out of her sanctum, exhaling explosively once outside to rid my lungs of the cloying scent of incense and decay that had surrounded her.

Before nightfall a contingent of palace clergy darkened our doorstep. Our village priestess accompanied them, cowering at their skirts like a submissive dog.

One of the women towered over the others. She stepped into our home and pushed back her cowl, revealing a smooth-shaven head and sharply defined features.

"I am Selene," she said in a deep, almost masculine voice. She nodded a greeting to my parents. I clutched the back of a chair and swallowed back bile. There was only one Selene in Fynia—the High Priestess. The scars on her bare forearms confirmed her rank, three deep parallel scratches from a captive gryphon's claws. She pointed a long, sharp-nailed forefinger at Nadia.

"Is this the one?"

Selene's every word made me swoon with fear, but Nadia seemed totally unaffected by her, for she stepped forward to meet her, tipped her head slightly backward, and said with that little smile that I would come to dread, "The baby shrivels in the Queen's womb. She will bear no more."

I closed my eyes to hold back the tears. What had I brought upon our family? Nadia was surely mad. They would take her away and lock her in an asylum. They would cut out her tongue for uttering such lunacies to a royal representative. They would execute us all and burn our house to the ground. They would...

I opened my eyes. Selene's hand rested on Nadia's shoulder and she smiled back at her in a way that loosened my bowels. Nadia blinked and frowned slightly, as if she were lost in an unfamiliar place. Selene looked over her head to my parents, who clung tightly to each other and shrunk into a corner.

"Your children are twins, yes?" She glanced at me, and I flinched as if whipped. My mother nodded.

"A boy and a girl," she mused. "One of them may be a Seer. And so beautiful..." She looked down at Nadia and stroked her cheek, and I had to stuff my fist in my mouth to stop myself from screaming.

"Your daughter could be very special," she said. "We must take her to the temple for assessment and training. You will, of course, be compensated." She made a tiny gesture, and her retinue parted to admit two soldiers bearing a freshly roasted suckling pig. Already my parents were advancing on it, their only children forgotten in their need to appease their empty bellies. Selene steered Nadia towards the door, then turned back and locked eyes with mine.

"We'll take the boy, too."

* * *

We married on our fourteenth birthday. I saw little of Nadia in the year leading up to our wedding day; Selene kept her busy with endless exercises designed to strengthen and control her ability. Selene soon discovered that I had no ability to See; besides some perfunctory lessons in royal history and etiquette, I was largely ignored, and I passed the time wandering the palace and temple alone. Occasionally I caught glimpses of Nadia, flanked on either side by two crimson-robed priestesses as they escorted her to some new ordeal. Each time

13

she looked a little smaller, a little paler, her smile becoming faint and bewildered before disappearing altogether.

True to Nadia's word, the Queen had nearly bled to death giving birth four months early to a tiny stillborn boy. Her physicians had pronounced her barren as a result, so the King and Queen adopted us, a solution that seemed ludicrous to me, with the Queen being barely five years older than us. Selene had found precedents in both religious and secular ancient documents that gave license to our adoption and marriage, despite their going against all natural laws. Had I been a man when we wed, I might have suffocated in an avalanche of emotions – pride, awe and trepidation at being elevated into the royal family, and revulsion at being used as breeding stock with my own sister to perpetuate the Seer bloodline. But I was still a child, so I felt only joy at the prospect of being reunited with my beloved Nadia.

We wept on our wedding night, clutching each other chastely in the darkness as we had always done before. And we wept the next night, I at the exquisite pleasure found in the act of physical love, and Nadia for reasons of her own. She had changed, my Nadia, her mind and her spirit, once twinned with mine, torn away and locked behind an invisible barricade as surely as her body was laid bare.

Once married, Nadia spewed forth prophecies, all of them accurate, and none of them happy news. She foresaw the death by poisoning of the King's brother and the subsequent war for possession of his lands; she predicted the storm that devastated most of Fynia's eastern fishing fleet; and she divined the exact nature of the malformation that would befall each of the seven children she bore. In accordance with divine law, we cast each pitiful twisted infant into the frigid waters of the river Tibus. Both the prophecies and the pregnancies sapped Nadia of her vitality, leaving her little more than a shell of a woman. I could not stand to be near her, to witness her deterioration, yet I could not abandon her to bear her pain alone. As much as I withdrew from her, she clung to me, insisting on a level of attention impossible to sustain, almost as if in punishment for the part I played in her misery. I would have given anything to lift the curse of her Sight from her, but the price was one that only she could pay.

* * *

I slip away from Nadia's chamber before she wakes. I feel ill, and it is not from the effects of the drink. I retire to my rooms. Perhaps this is my destiny, to die drenched in a fever and huddled in my bed like a feeble old man. I contemplate summoning a physician, when someone hammers frantically on my door.

"Prince Malik! Come quickly! There has been an accident... Princess Nadia..."

The sick feeling in my stomach intensifies, swirling out from my belly and setting off tremors in my limbs. I have been a self-absorbed fool; she did not predict my death, she predicted her own. I leap out of bed and run, skidding down the hall, after the servant who has summoned me. He leads me to her chamber. The room is awash with people. They are all talking at once, and I cannot understand what any of them are saying. A white silk curtain billows gently in the open doorway to Nadia's balcony. A trail of blood leads from the balcony to the bed. I elbow my way through the throng to the bedside. A trio of physicians huddles over Nadia's prone body. I shove them aside.

She is weeping blood. Two deep vertical gouges mark where her eyes used to be. *I will not see you again.* The pieces fall appallingly into place. I take her into my arms.

"I called a gryphon," she whispers. "It spoke to me. I gave it my Sight in return."

My tears fall onto her ravaged face, and she smiles at me, a genuine smile that creases the corners of her empty sockets. The expression is both grotesque and beautiful.

"Don't cry, Malik," she says, her fingers unerringly caressing my cheek. "It was a good trade."

Side Show Sally

She has a way of frightening
even the most foolhardy
with her bed-of-nails beauty.
Sandwiched between
the clown and the strong man,
she passes time between meals
filing tooth and claw to points.
She blinks her tiny eye
and turns around twice
in pursuit of her own tail.
The ladies swoon; their escorts
catch them while measuring
the distance to the door.

Becoming

Geena's fingers ached with the strain of bearing her weight as she clung to the edge of the precipice. She scrabbled for a foothold against the cliff face, sending dirt and pebbles showering down onto the rocks far below her. Any moment now her strength would give out, and she would follow them.

"Papa, please! Pull me up! I'm going to fall!"

Papa stood above her, silhouetted against the sun, his face contorted in anger. The light cast a corona about his head, making him look like a vengeful god. Geena blinked away tears and fought to focus on Mama, who stood behind Papa's left shoulder.

"Marcus, for pity's sake, pull her up!" Mama pleaded. "She's just a baby!"

Papa rounded on her. "She's not a baby! She's fifteen! If you hadn't continued to treat her like a baby these past few years, it might not have come to this."

"Mama...," Geena called. Her fingers were slipping. Her mother moved towards her, but Papa flung out his arm and forced her back. Mama covered her face with her hands and sobbed.

"Fifteen years old," Papa muttered to himself, "and look at her. All the others long since flown...how did I produce a child so weak?" He crouched in front of Geena, suddenly looking weary beyond his years, and reached a hand out to her. She smiled with relief. He was going to relent and pull her up after all.

And then, one by one, he prized her fingers free.

The rushing wind tore Geena's scream from her throat. She closed her eyes against the sight of the ground rising up to meet her. Pain blossomed in her shoulder blades and radiated outwards through her body. It was worse than her friends had described to her, it was all she had feared and more, and it consumed her utterly.

She felt a massive wrenching in her back and her body jerked suddenly upwards. Her head whipped back and forth with the jolt and her teeth clamped on her tongue, drawing blood. She hung breathless in the air for a moment, and then slowly rose.

She opened her eyes. Her newly sprouted wings extended six feet on either side of her. They were a rich charcoal grey, just like her father's, and they glistened in the sun as they beat, rhythmic and steady, powered by millennia of instinctive knowledge flowing through her veins.

Her parents extended their wings and leapt from the cliff to join her. Papa hovered at her side and spoke the ritual words of Becoming. Mama, tearful but smiling, took Geena's hands in her own and leaned forward to kiss her on the cheek.

"You see?" Papa said. "I told you it would work." He was right, as always, and Geena yearned with a surge of rebellion as fresh as her wings to dash away his smug look of triumph.

But that could wait for another time. She turned her face skyward, flexed her muscles, and soared.

The Last Tiger

This story started as an experiment using a second person point of view. It was first published in Electric Velocipede #14, an issue of women writers compiled for release at Wiscon, the world's leading feminist-oriented science fiction and fantasy convention.

Hunger has made you reckless. You track the sound of human voices through the woods until you find a man and a woman. They are shouting at each other. The woman slaps the man's face. He presses his hand to his cheek for a moment, and then lunges at the woman, knocking her to the ground. He squeezes his hands tight about her throat. The noises she makes are ugly.

Your nostrils flare. You smell food. It is in the pack on the man's back. You come closer to the couple, deliberately snapping a twig underfoot. The man whirls around, almost losing his grip on the woman.

You point at the back pack.

"Food," you say. You have to concentrate on forming the words correctly, your voice husky and harsh from lack of use. "Give it." The man stands, releasing the woman. She scuttles backward, sobbing and gasping in air over bruised vocal chords. Two words enter your head, and you ponder their meaning.

Civilian. Combatant.

The man pulls a hunting knife from his back pocket. Stepping forward, he brandishes the knife inches from your face.

"You gonna make me, sweetheart?" he says.

Civilian. Combatant. His knife is like a flipping switch. You try to remember what to do, but there is a roaring sound in your ears, and your

19

vision clouds over in a red fog. When it clears, it is already done. Your muscles ache and you are breathing heavily, as if you have run a long distance. The switchblade is dripping blood onto the man's corpse. You flip him over with your foot and crouch to open the back pack. You eat quickly, alert for competitors.

The woman still sits a few feet away, hugging her knees to her chest. She speaks to you, and you ignore her, concentrating on your meal. She is a Civilian, of no interest or threat to you. She tilts her head to the side, inviting you to respond. When you do not, she stands, shifting her weight from foot to foot and looking around her in agitation. Her words become louder, more abrupt and more insistent. You have finished eating, so you rise and turn to leave.

"Wait," she says. "Food."

You stop.

"Come with me, and I can get you more food. As much as you want."

She beckons to you, her eyes wide and pleading like a rabbit caught in a trap just before you break its neck. You can barely remember the last time you caught a rabbit. She takes a few tentative steps, still beckoning, and you follow.

* * *

Grace, Ethan and the Prof stood at one end of the kitchen, their eyes fixed on the woman at the other end. She was dressed in a filthy mini dress that might once have been red, a fleece-lined camouflage jacket with the sales tags still showing, and what looked and smelled like the hide of two small furry animals crudely tied fur side in to her feet. Standing, she was nearly six feet tall, but now she was squatting on the floor, balancing a large dinner plate in one hand and shovelling rice and beans into her mouth with the other.

Her subsistence diet had stripped her body to the bare essentials, her long bones bound in ropy muscle. Her hair and her skin were the same shade of tawny brown. With her delicate features, expressionless face, and hair that jutted from her skull in unevenly cropped clumps, she looked like an over-sized, misused and discarded doll.

"Ethan wanted to turn her in right away," said Grace, "but I said we should wait for you."

"Of course I wanted to turn her in!" said Ethan. "Do you know the penalty for harbouring one of those?" He jerked his head in the direction of the woman.

"You don't even know if she is 'one of those'!" said Grace. "What do you think, Prof–is she Enhanced?"

"Based on what you told me, I'd say she is. No normal human being could move as fast as you said she did. See that scar on her leg?" He pointed out a puckered indentation the size of a baby's fist on the woman's right thigh. "That was probably where her military ident chip was. She would have dug it out herself."

Grace winced. "What will they do to her if we turn her in?"

"I expect they will strap her down, conduct several weeks of excruciatingly painful tests on her, and then kill her," said the Prof.

"But we can't let them do that! She saved my life!"

Ethan took Grace by the shoulders, forcing her to face him. "Grace, honey–she can't stay here. Even if the cops don't get wind of it, she's dangerous. She could turn on us any minute."

"Ethan's right about one thing," said the Prof. "She's about as safe and predictable as a lightly tethered tiger."

"So what are we going to do with her?" said Ethan.

"It's not up to us," said the Prof. "She'll do what she wants to do. My guess is she'll fuel up, take as many provisions as she can carry and go back into hiding. I suggest we try not to get in her way. It's best for all concerned," he said, patting Grace on the shoulder. "In the meantime, there's the small matter of a dead body in the woods. You two had better get rid of it before someone finds it and comes asking awkward questions. I'll sort things out here with our guest."

* * *

The one they call The Prof is right. You did make that mark on your leg, a long, long time ago, when you were smaller and weaker and more frightened of the Men With Guns then you were of the pain. He is right about many things.

You wonder if he is right about the tiger. You don't know what a tiger is, but you like the sound of it. You run the word through your head—tigertigertiger–and imagine a large, powerful animal loping, silent and invisible, through the sun-dappled undergrowth.

There is something familiar about the Prof. You have not met him before, but you have known others like him, others who carried themselves the same way, who spoke and were obeyed in the same way. The Designers. Part of you wants to submit to him, to prostrate yourself at his feet and beg for his guidance, and part of you wants to snap his neck where he stands.

"I'm going to leave now," he says, "but I will be back soon with some supplies for you to take. Food, blankets, tools, that sort of thing. Wait here. You will be safe."

You check the door after he has left. It opens freely. He told you to wait. So you wait.

* * *

The Prof threw down a laden pack and swore. The kitchen was empty. With a resigned sigh, he turned to leave, when he caught a flicker of movement out of the corner of his eye. The woman emerged from another room.

"Computer," she said in a flat, croaky voice. "I find... tiger." She held up a printout showing a photo of a tiger bounding through long grass in pursuit of a deer.

"You remember how to read and type?" he said.

"I remember... many things." She advanced slowly through the kitchen towards him, brushing her hand over the walls, the table top, a coffee cup, her lips moving as she sub-vocalised the objects' names.

"I always wanted to meet someone like you," he said. "Call it professional curiosity. I applied to join the military GE team, but they turned me down, despite, I must add, the fact that I was widely acknowledged to be one of the finest minds in the field. Something about my psychological profile being unsuitable. Then the Greenies got into power, and those stinking tree-hugging Luddites shut everyone down. Decades of research, destroyed overnight."

"I've still got it, though. Most of my findings are right here," he said, tapping his temple. "There's a good chance this government won't last another term, and with the right stuff to give me a head start I could be implanting viable embryos inside a year. So I wonder if I could trouble you for some of your DNA. A few strands of hair, some skin scrapings, maybe a little blood...?"

The woman answered him only with her impassive gaze. He shrugged. "I suppose you haven't understood a word I've said. No matter–I'll probably find enough shed material in this room to make do." He looked away, his words now only for his own ears. "If I pull it off, they'll be hailing me as the father of the next generation."

The woman frowned. She looked from the Prof to the paper in her hand and back again.

"Father?" she said.

* * *

Even with the heavy pack on your back, you make good time, reaching the edge of the woods just before nightfall. The lengthening shadows cast pleasing stripes across your body. A thick plume of smoke bisects the skyline behind you, the result of your handiwork.

There will be no shed material for the Prof to collect. And there is no longer a Prof to collect it. You take a printed sheet of paper from your pocket and read it for the seventeenth time.

'Tiger fathers are a threat to the cubs and may even attempt to kill them.'

Not if you strike first.

Nim of the Kamankay

This was the first of my stories to appear in a print anthology. My level of excitement at the time is reflected in the number of surplus copies I purchased and which still sit on my bookshelf. Nim and her band of merry mercenaries make a repeat appearance in "Dark Wing", and you might recognize Maeve as a relative of Nim's in "On The Border".

Nim's leather battle skirt slapped against her heavily muscled thighs as she strode into the marketplace. She had not visited Illac for several years, not since she was a fourteen year old on her first campaign, but the layout of these marketplaces was all much the same. She stopped to buy a meal from a street vendor, thick slices of wild boar cut from a slowly turning spit and served between two slabs of bread, and slowed to an amble as she approached the Mercenary Quarter.

From the opposite side of a wide, dusty track, she studied the bands of mercenaries touting their skills, discounting the first few almost immediately. One looked to consist of rank amateurs, inexperienced farm boys full of bravado and not much else. They'd probably wet their pants in a real battle, she thought. Others appeared battle-hardened on the surface, but Nim noticed that they used their time inefficiently. Some gambled, some drank copious amounts of the harsh, potent local brew, some slipped off into their tents with a camp whore or two, and some just lay in the sun and dozed.

Then she spotted a small band, maybe a dozen men, with potential. They looked little different from the others to a casual observer, but Nim noticed they were all engaged in various forms of battle preparation. Those not occupied with mending gear and sharpening weapons were sparring, honing their skills and reflexes. They were a motley lot, ranging in age, size and colour, but they all looked fit, strong and fast.

Nim studied them closer, looking for the leader. Not the one grooming the horses, she thought – he was too young. Not the tall one, either, his black ponytail flicking through the air as he moved through an intricate kata – he was too absorbed in himself to be overseeing others. What about the big fellow with the bushy red beard, the one sharpening a double-headed axe and bellowing with laughter at one of his comrade's jokes? No, too obvious - he was probably the decoy leader.

There. A man of medium height and medium build strolled amongst the men, pausing to offer words of encouragement or admonishment to sparring partners, test the edges of newly honed swords, and haggle with the armourers and horse traders mingling with the warriors.

Nim swallowed her last mouthful of boar and crossed the road. She planted herself in front of the man. "I'm looking for a job," she said.

Several of the mercenaries looked around at the sound of her voice. Some guffawed loudly, while others stared in open-mouthed amazement. The leader, however, was unmoved. He looked up at her with sea-grey eyes. "And you are...?"

Before she could answer, the big redheaded man pushed his way to the troupe leader's side. "Look, lassie," he said, "we've already got a Healer, and Davad over there," he indicated the young man attending to the horses, "is the best cook this side of the Arctian Mountains." He looked her slowly up and down, and continued, "And you're far too ugly to be a camp whore." The gathering audience sniggered and nudged each other.

Nim looked him over in a deliberate parody of the inspection he had just given her. "How fortunate for me," she said, then turned her attention back to the leader.

"My name's Nim," she said, extending a calloused hand. He didn't move. "Nim?" he said softly, raising an eyebrow. "The name's a little... small to fit you, isn't it?"

Nim flushed. "My full name is Nimue," she muttered. The leader studied her, taking in her broad cheekbones and heavy chin, her coarse black hair cropped short above her shoulders, the dusty sleeveless jerkin displaying biceps bigger than those of most of his men, and the holster bristling with weapons slung across her wide back.

"Nim it is," he said, suppressing a smile. "My name is Zak. Well, Nim, if you want to join us, you'll have to prove yourself first. What do you say, Grilt?" he said, turning to the redhead. "Care to give us a demonstration match with Nim here? Defender has choice of weapons."

Someone drew a makeshift ring in the dirt. Bystanders from other camps began to amble over, eager for some relief from boredom. A buxom woman of indeterminate years with a heavily painted face fished a coin purse from her cleavage and started taking bets. Grilt's patronising grin widened. He hefted his battle axe. "Ever used one of these, lassie?"

In Nim's experience, men the size of Grilt fell into two categories. Either they were gentle giants, unused to physical conflict because few were brave or foolhardy enough to challenge them, or else they revelled in it, falsely assuming that their sheer brute strength was all they needed to guarantee a victory. Grilt's choice of weapon placed him squarely in the latter group. A two-headed axe was impractical for a demonstration-only fight. It was big and heavy and looked intimidating, but was almost impossible to wield with any finesse. Almost.

The man they called Davad pressed an axe into her hands. Grilt began to warm up, lobbing his axe from hand to hand as easily as if it were an apple. With a flourish, he tossed it over his shoulder and caught it behind his back. A ragged cheer rippled through the audience. He gave an exaggerated bow to Nim, sweeping his hand before him to give her leave to emulate him, if she dared. Her face remained impassive, but inwardly she smiled. She held the handle of the axe in a two-fisted grip, and began to spin it. Faster and faster it rotated, sunlight flashing off the blade, until it was a blur of wood and steel whistling through the air. With a flick of her wrist, she tossed it skyward. It arced lazily to the peak of its ascent, seemed to hover for an instant, and then plummeted back to earth. A split second before the blade could connect with her skull, she sidestepped, catching the handle in her left hand.

The audience gasped. There was a flurry of nervous activity around the doxy taking bets. Grilt's smile faltered. He spat on both hands, crouched slightly and scraped his foot twice in the dust, like a bull about to charge. With a low growl, he ran at her, swinging his weapon. Nim easily parried his opening attacks. She noted that, with each blow, Grilt would rotate the axe at the end of his swing so that she was only ever facing the flat of the blade. He also kept his attacks below head level. The worst she could expect, should any of his blows land on her, would be some nasty bruises and perhaps a broken bone or two. It showed discipline and a respect for his craft that he would take such steps to avoid maiming or killing a sparring opponent. She had made the right choice in approaching this band of mercenaries.

Not that Nim intended to be quite as gallant as Grilt. She leant backwards in a blur of movement to avoid a couple of sweeping attacks, then parried the next two, allowing the two blades to clang against each other for the spectators' benefit. As Grilt leant his considerable weight against hers, she put her leading foot against his and twisted her body to the side. Suddenly deprived of any resistance, he sprawled forward into the dirt. Nim swung her axe alarmingly close to his face, neatly slicing off two inches of beard.

The audience roared with laughter. Grilt stared at the remains of his beard, dead in the dust like some small russet animal. His eyes widened until it seemed that they were going to pop out of his head. Snorting and snarling, he scrambled to his feet and rushed at Nim, fists flying and axe forgotten. So much for discipline and respect, Nim thought. He swung a roundhouse punch at her head, which she smoothly evaded. As the momentum of his swing carried him past her, she tapped him on the back of his skull with the flat of her blade. Grilt swayed on his feet for a few agonising seconds before his eyes rolled back in his head and his legs gave way beneath him.

The crowd was silent for a moment, and then erupted into cheers. Nim was buffeted by countless congratulatory slaps on the back. The successful betters collected their winnings. The bookie shook her coin purse, now much slimmer than before, in Nim's direction and gave a wry smile. An older woman with short-cropped grey hair and wearing men's breeches elbowed her way through to the centre of the ring and crouched beside the still-prone Grilt. She probed his skull and neck with expert fingers, lifted each of his eyelids, then looked up at Zak standing nearby.

"He'll live," she said. "You, you, you and you," pointing out four nearby members of the troupe, "take a limb each and put him in the shade. His head is going to be hurting badly enough as it is when he comes around without adding sunstroke to his injuries. And as for you," she said, addressing Nim, "now that you're one of us, you'll be drawing double duties. This was meant to be my day off." Her tone was grim, but she tipped Nim a wink as she marched off after her patient, who was just beginning to groan and stir as his comrades jostled him to safety.

Nim turned to Zak. He extended his hand, and they clasped each other's forearms in a gesture of equals. "Well fought, Nim," he said, "although you might have made one tactical error. When Grilt wakes up, he'll be pestering you for days on how you made that sidestep." His expression turned serious. "You're Kamankayan, aren't you?" She nodded. "You're a long way from home. I thought Kamankayans never left their tribe."

"My reasons for leaving my tribe need not concern you," Nim said.

"That's good to hear," replied Zak. "You'll find the members of our little group to be fiercely loyal to each other, despite the fact that they're paid to be here. But if you bring any trouble down on us," he said, his voice low and emphatic, "they will not hesitate to rip you apart."

"You sound as though you know a little about my people," Nim said. "Yes, they might come looking for me. They might even find me. But they like to keep their business to themselves. So long as nobody tried to interfere, they would pluck me from your midst as cleanly as plucking a feather from a goose's tail."

Zak nodded. "I've seen a Kamankayan unit at work. Never had to come up against one, of course, otherwise I would probably be dead. I believe what you say." He put an arm around Nim's shoulder and steered her towards his camp. "Come on," he said, "after the display you just put on, I think you deserve an ale. But mind you have only one. You've got work to do."

Sun Stands Still

They feast and dance
And stoke the fires
To vanquish the
child-eating God
of Gloom.

Yet there is one
Who honours still
the Dark.

She sits alone
And cold and quiet,
Shaping resentments
And regrets
Into a living thing.

At the instant
Of the Solstice
She gives birth to
A grotesquerie.

It spreads its wings
And red maw wide,
Devours its dam,
And the Sun
Stands still.

Baptism

I wrote the poem "Sleeping with the Fishes" about a mermaid living in a back yard pool, but I had a feeling that I wasn't finished with her yet. Nor was she finished with me. Then I read the controversial book "This Horrid Practice" by Paul Moon, detailing the history of cannibalism amongst pre-European New Zealand Maori, and how the arrival of the missionaries quickly eradicated the practice.

In "On Writing," Stephen King talks about story ideas "sailing at you right out of the empty sky: two previously unrelated ideas come together and make something new under the sun." The ideas for this story didn't exactly come from nowhere, but they were definitely unrelated, at least until my subconscious got hold of them and shook them up together.

Brother Tomas drew his habit tightly around himself, a futile gesture against the biting sea wind. He eyed the tiny island in the middle of the bay that would be his new home. He had been in Koreka for less than a half a day, and already he was homesick for the Secoduna Desert. His superiors had decreed that he be sent here, and they took their instruction directly from God, but sometimes he wondered if they might not occasionally be mistaken in their interpretation. Have faith, Brother, he silently chastised himself. Surely, this was no mistake; if anyone could succeed where others had failed, it would be him.

"You're the fourth friar I've rowed out there in as many months," said Mellie, the rawboned young woman who had been assigned as his escort. She gripped the oars with two windchapped, meaty hands and leaned back, sending the little boat surging against the wavelets. "But

I didn't row any of them back, not alive, leastways. What makes you think you'll do better?"

"Greater experience, true devotion to and faith in Our Lord, and a plentiful supply of chasteberry tea." Tomas smiled and patted his rucksack. His smile faded as he sniffed the air. "What's that smell?"

Mellie looked over her shoulder. A large log bobbed in the water several feet away. Mellie grinned humourlessly and rowed harder until they grew level with the object. A ripe, overwhelming stench rose from it. The 'log' had a face.

The corpse floated on its back, its eye sockets empty and its mouth open to the sky. It still wore its shirt, cravat and jacket, but was naked from the waist down. Its groin was a ragged mess of tattered, bloodless flesh. Tomas retched and covered his mouth and nose with his sleeve.

"What's the matter, Brother?" said Mellie. "Haven't you ever seen a dead man before?"

"I've dealt with many bodies, but they were all..."

"Less chewed?"

"I was going to say 'drier'."

"You'd better get used to it. Most of them wash up on your island." Mellie picked up a pike, hooked it through the dead man's shirt and dragged it to the side of the boat. With a grunt, she hauled it over the side and dropped it at Tomas's feet, sending up a fresh miasma of decay.

"They all think they can withstand the lure of the mermaids' song. We try to warn them, but..." She shook her head.

"...but if you tried too hard, it might be bad for business," Tomas finished. With all the able-bodied menfolk of the town either dead or moved away, their traditional livelihood of fishing was defunct, their nets left to rot on the shore. Perversely, the town thrived, their boats converted from functional fishing vessels to pleasure craft as men flocked from all parts of the country. Most came seeking to satisfy their prurient curiosity, some came to challenge themselves, but save for a few wretched suicides, they all expected to live to tell the tale.

But Tomas was not here for those misguided men. He was here to save the mermaids' immortal souls.

As if in response to his thoughts, a dozen sleek heads broke the surface of the water within arm's length of the boat. Mellie hissed and smacked at the mermaids with her oar. They hissed back and retreated to a safer distance.

"They like to hang around and gloat when we bring in a body, the filthy bitches." She spat into the sea. Her spittle rested for an instant on the surface before dissipating. "Pardon my language, Brother."

Tomas barely heard her. He crossed himself as the mermaids encircled the boat, his eyes never leaving them. He had been told that there were no mermen, and that in the absence of available human partners, mermaids coupled with other sea creatures. Indeed, he could see evidence of this in their features; one had a fat round face that bristled with spikes, suggesting that she had been sired by a puffer fish. Another, with her tiny little black eyes set wide on either side of an elongated face, was undoubtedly the offspring of a shark. The impression intensified as she opened her mouth and gave a gurgling approximation of a human laugh, displaying three rows of razor sharp teeth.

He had also been told that, even when they were not singing, the mermaids exuded a malignant glamour, and that to be in close proximity with one was to experience temptation on an almost unbearable scale. His manhood stiffened and pressed against his breechclout, and he shuffled painfully in his seat, anxious to conceal it from Mellie. He had resisted the advances of many a bejewelled Secoduna beauty, yet one look at these creatures and he had to grip the sides of the boat to stop from flinging himself into the water.

"A new man of God!" the shark-like one said. Her voice bubbled like slow-boiling porridge, and Tomas's stomach roiled. "I do hope you will be as... entertaining as the last ones." Her tail undulated, propelling her torso above the water's surface, and she flung back her long black hair to thrust her breasts at him.

Nobody had told him about the gills.

A line of red-tinged slits ran down each flank, pulsating gently in time to the rise and fall of the mermaid's chest. He clutched his rosary beads, closed his eyes and muttered a fervent prayer.

"You're wasting your time," said Mellie. "Praying isn't going to save you–ask any widow in Koreka. The mermaids aren't children of God, they're the spawn of the Devil. And the sooner the Church realises that, the sooner you can stop trying to save their souls and start exterminating them like the vermin they are." She scowled and bent again to her rowing.

"I'd better get you to your island. It's nearly sundown, and I've still got a corpse to bury."

* * *

Tomas's island sloped sharply upwards to a peak in its centre, too steep for him to climb unaided. It was covered in drab, low-lying fruitless scrub, and took less than an hour for him to circumnavigate on foot. Based on the reports from his predecessors, Tomas expected the mermaids to immediately commence a campaign to seduce him, but for several days he was left alone. The only evidence of their presence was a daily offering of freshly caught fish left on the end of the small jetty near his hut. It was while he was collecting this gift one morning that the mermaids resurfaced, by which time he was almost glad to see them.

"Good morning, ladies," he said, inclining his head, and taking care to stand out of reach of their taloned hands. "My name is Brother Tomas Santoyo. Might I enquire as to your names?" The arousal he had felt when he first encountered them washed over him anew. He swayed slightly, dizzy and weak-kneed with lust.

The shark-faced one, evidently their leader, swam forward. She held a hunk of flesh in one hand, and from time to time took delicate bites from it. Tomas could not tell what kind of meat it was.

"My name is Sh'Teth," she said. She named the others in rapid-fire, sibilant mertongue.

"And who is that?" Tomas indicated a small fair-haired mermaid a short distance away at the back of the pod.

"Her? Oh, she is nobody—just a slave we captured."

The mermaid in question swam forward. Unlike most of the others, she looked strikingly like a human female. Whipped by the wind, her fine hair was already almost dry, revealing itself to be a fetching golden blonde. Her father must have been a handsome man, God rest his soul, thought Tomas. The mermaid looked up at him with wide blue eyes. As she bobbed in the water, Tomas noticed that her belly was swollen, evidently in the later stages of pregnancy.

"Basha," she said. "My name is Basha."

Sh'Teth snarled, spun on Basha, and struck a vicious open-handed blow across her face. She growled something in mertongue that made the smaller mermaid cringe and retreat, clutching a bleeding bottom lip.

"Pay no attention to her," said Sh'Teth, waving her gory repast at Tomas. "She is lucky we let her live."

"What are you eating?" he asked.

"Baby," she replied. She held the meat outstretched to him on her two upturned palms. "Would you like some?"

At first, he thought that he had misheard her. Then he saw a small white bone protruding from one end of the offering, three tiny fingers on the other, and two pink oozing stumps where the missing digits should be. The blood drained from his face. He stumbled backward in horror and dropped to his hands and knees on the deck. He dug his fingers into the boards and retched.

"Please tell me that child was already dead when you found it," he gasped.

"Of course it wasn't," said Sh'Teth, looking offended. "We are hunters, not scavengers. We took it from another pod last night."

"Then it's not...not human?"

"Oh, Brother Tomas, we would never eat a human baby. That would be a sin."

For a moment Tomas felt a glimmer of hope. If the mermaids had some concept of sin, even a grotesquely distorted concept such as this, then perhaps his predecessors' work had not been entirely in vain.

The mermaids burst into laughter. They were making sport of their heinous crime, and what was worse, they were mocking him. He raised his head and watched, his eyes filled with tears, as they slapped the water with their tails and swam away. Only Basha did not laugh. She trailed behind the others and looked back at him, her face incandescent with sorrow.

* * *

Tomas sat on the end of the jetty and swung his legs like a child. He closed his eyes and turned his face up to the sun. It was moments like these, quiet and pure and simple, when he could almost feel the presence of God.

Almost.

A familiar flood of lust washed over him, and he opened his eyes to see just a gleaming head. No, two heads, he thought with a smile–Basha held a tiny merbaby in her arms. The child was golden-haired, like her mother. Her chubby little hands flailed against Basha's breast as she suckled noisily. Basha swam in tight circles just out of reach of the end of the jetty and made a nervous humming noise in the back of her throat.

"What is it, Basha?"

"I'm not supposed to be here," she said. "If Sh'teth knew..."

"Well, then, we won't tell her." He smiled to reassure her. "Congratulations on the birth of your baby. She is beautiful. What have you named her?"

"That is why I have come to you. The last Brother said that if we were to baptise our babies, then they would go to Heaven." She lowered her head to gaze lovingly at her child. "I like the sound of Heaven," she said, her voice barely louder than a whisper. "It sounds so much better than here."

"I would be honoured to do so," said Tomas. "But she will need a good Christian name. I think I shall call her Constance."

Basha swam closer and held the baby up to Tomas. She was so close to him now, close to enough to touch, and he only had to throw his weight forward a little more to join her in the water...

She all but threw her baby into his arms and hastily swam away, as if she feared his touch would burn. Tomas let out a breath, grateful for the minor respite from Basha's glamour. He scooped up handfuls of sea water to sprinkle over the baby's head.

"Constance, I baptize you in the Name of the Father, and of the Son, and of the Holy Spirit."

He felt a little like a fisherman releasing an undersized catch as he lowered the wriggling infant into the sea and sent her swimming back to her mother.

* * *

Tomas had been on the island for five months, a new record for Koreka missionaries, and he had received a letter from the bishop congratulating him for his piety and fortitude. But Tomas was not celebrating; the mermaids were singing tonight. A string of lights bobbed in the bay as a small flotilla of boats set sail from the mainland to meet them. Most of the men aboard would be bound to a post to prevent them from jumping overboard, but there were always a few wanting to pit their will against the mermaids'. No doubt Tomas would be towing their mangled corpses up the beach in a few days' time.

Sighing, he turned back to his scriptures. He could not sleep while the mermaids sang. He drank chasteberry tea until his tongue was stained blue, stuffed his ears with wads of cotton against their high-pitched wordless wail, and prayed until his knees were bruised, yet still he shook with the effort of keeping his feet on the sand. When they finally fell silent, he knew his dreams would be plagued with visions of their inviting arms, their high, pale breasts, their throbbing, incarnadine gills...

He shook himself like a dog shedding water. The words in front of him ran together into nonsense. He pushed the book aside. It hit the floor, sending up a small cloud of dust. He left it where it lay and took up a pen and parchment.

Dear Bishop Lucian

Thank you for your recent letter. Your words of faith and encouragement were most welcome to me. However, I have come to the conclusion that our mission here at Koreka is one of greatest folly.

Despite the mermaids' superficial resemblance to human women, and their facility with the English language, my work has led me to believe that they are more of the order of beasts of the field and the jungle than of fully sentient creatures capable of receiving the full Grace of God. Some of the mermaids show evidence of intelligence, comparable even to their feminine two-legged counterparts, and I have been able to engage in some rudimentary theological discussions with them. Perhaps, in time, I might even be able to dissuade them from some of their more abhorrent practices, such as their aggression towards other mermaid pods and their cannibalistic tendencies. Regrettably, it is their means of reproduction that provides the greatest barrier to salvation. Their base nature compels them to seek profane unions with human men, and occasionally lesser sea creatures. They have rejected all attempts to persuade them to live in holy matrimony, and with good reason; removed from the sea, they fail to thrive, and pine away to death in a matter of months. And of course, it is impossible for a human man to live in their environment. They are no more capable of choosing a life of chastity and fidelity than the wolf is capable of choosing not to eat the lamb.

I therefore request that the Koreka mission be closed down, and that I be assigned to a new post where I might be more usefully employed in the service of our Lord.

Your humble servant,

Brother Tomas Santoyo

Tomas read over his letter. He had held high hopes for converting Basha, but since the baptism, she had kept her distance from him, as if she were afraid that he might betray her to the rest of the pod. Surely, he thought, this was the most sensible course of action, for himself, for the Church, for the mermaids… yet he hesitated before putting his seal upon the letter.

Perhaps the mermaids *did* need him. Perhaps he was all that stood in the way of their certain extermination. For if his superiors were to believe his account and were to reconsider the mermaids' status, they surely would not suffer them to live. As much as he despised the mermaids' way of life, he was not prepared to sign their death warrant.

A loud female voice, clearly audible even through his ear plugs, shook him from his reverie.

"Tomas! Please, Tomas, help me!"

Tomas tore the cotton from his ears, snatched up a lamp, and ran outside. He clattered down the jetty and skidded to a halt. Basha clung to the boards. Deep scratches striped her face and body, her blood glistening almost black in the flickering lamp light.

"We were attacked by another pod... the others escaped, but I was too slow... Tomas, they killed Constance!"

"Oh, Basha..."

Her pain and despair was palpable. Without thinking, Tomas prostrated himself on the jetty and wrapped an arm around her shoulders, drawing her into an awkward embrace. He sought only to comfort her, but the touch of his skin on hers intensified the mermaid's allure beyond his ability to resist. He turned his head and pressed his open mouth to hers. His heart seemed to stop in his chest as she returned his kiss.

Then she grabbed him by the shoulders and pulled. She was strong, freakishly strong, and he offered no resistance as he slid into the water. He clasped Basha to him, and their combined weight dragged them slowly down. Basha wriggled away from him, and he had a moment to consider how lovely her hair looked as it swirled about her in the gentle current, another moment to wonder how it was that he could see her, underwater and in the dark, and then he was shooting skyward.

He drew a deep, shuddering breath as he broke the surface. His lamp had tipped over and set the jetty alight. The heat from the mermaid's kiss flowed outward from his lips to infuse his entire body, mirroring the fire. The flames cast a ruddy glow over the water as they licked at the spilt oil and raced along the boards.

It was if he were seeing fire for the first time. The flames bowed and pirouetted, seguing from the palest yellow to vivid orange to arterial red, their own hushed roar the song to which they danced. The sea lapped gently at his shoulders, caressing him through his sodden robes as he trod water. He inhaled again, savouring the scented air. Salt, seaweed, sagebrush, burning pitch, he could distinguish each aroma, yet it all combined into an exquisite perfume. Now he understood why so many men risked death to embrace the mermaids; in one instant Basha had changed him. She had brought him anew into the world, immersed him in sensation, she had...

She had brought him closer to God.

He wept. Basha came to him to drink his tears, catching each drop on the tip of her tongue. The sea rippled around him in a dozen different places as Sh'teth and her pod rose to take their turns embracing him. In the dimmest regions of his lust-fogged mind, he wondered if they had used Basha as bait to lure him into the water. Once this would have enraged him, but now it no longer seemed to matter.

He wept as the mermaids' caresses became more insistent. They tugged and tore at his robe and undergarments until he floated naked, and they adorned him with their own bare flesh. He wept as they took their pleasure of him, holding him submerged until he reached the brink of unconsciousness, then allowing him the briefest of respites before dragging him under again. He wept as his own climaxes ripped him apart and reassembled him in strange new ways. Even as the mermaids took him down for the final time, he wept, although whether it was from the agony or the ecstasy, he could not tell.

* * *

The boat sat low in the water under Brother Alton's weight. With every lurch of the oars, water splashed over the sides, soaking the hem of his habit.

"Don't know why you're bothering," said his escort. "You can't convert the mermaids, and there are four gravestones on that island to prove it. I hear Brother Tomas even wrote a letter to the bishop telling him so—right before he died."

"If such a letter exists, then it is the property of the church, and no business of yours," he said. "In any case, Brother Tomas was weak, just like the others." He jabbed at his chest with a podgy forefinger. "Whereas I will prevail."

She raised one eyebrow, and seemed about to say something, when there was a disturbance in the water off the prow of the boat. Alton half-stood to see what it was, sending the boat rocking.

"Welcome to Koreka, Brother," said the thing in the water.

Alton sat slack-jawed and speechless. Nothing he had read or heard about the mermaids could have prepared him for this. She was beautiful, she was terrible, she was completely, unmercifully compelling. As she lifted her body above the waves, he could already feel himself drowning.

House Arrest

"Angela! Darling! You look marvellous!"

The women flashed carnivorous smiles as they waved a greeting to the newcomer. Angela tottered on needle-like heels to the nearest available seat and collapsed into it, pressing the back of her skeletal hand to her forehead.

"Why, thank you, darlings," she said. "But you know, it's been a nightmare. An absolute nightmare. I wouldn't wish it on anyone."

"We knew something terrible must have happened when you didn't show up to Tariq's party," said Leonie. "It was the social event of the year. Do tell, darling – where have you been? You weren't... arrested, were you?"

"You could say that," said Angela, her bottom lip quivering, "but it's not what you think. It was my house. It wouldn't let me out."

"No, darling!"

"Yes, darlings!" she replied. "I asked it for a little assistance with my weight loss programme, and it got carried away. I thought at first that it was just a minor fault in the system, when it disconnected the phone every time I tried to call out for pizza. Then the fridge and pantry doors locked up, and I couldn't get into them unless I ran for an hour on the treadmill. And then, when I threatened to call in a technician, the house locked the doors and shut down the phone. I was trapped, darlings!"

She was warming to her audience, the honed edges of her synthetic fingernails glinting in the dim light as she gestured theatrically.

"What did you do? How did you escape?"

"Well, what could I do? I had to subsist on limp rocket leaves and Evian water until I registered the correct weight on my bathroom scales, and it let me go. I haven't been back since."

"Have they managed to fix it yet?" asked Charlene.

Angela shook her head. "I'm still staying in a hotel. Luckily it's covered by insurance. Nobody has been able to get near the CPU–the house keeps zapping them. One technician was even hospitalised. If they don't get to the root of the problem soon, they're talking about condemning the apartment."

Five pairs of mascara-framed eyes widened in horror. "No,darling!"

"Yes, darlings!"

The women contemplated Angela's emaciated frame. Charlene was first to break the silence.

"Darling," she whispered, leaning over and patting Angela's bony knee, "before that happens...do you think I could borrow your apartment key?"

Killing a Goddess

Yes, gentle reader, sometimes story ideas do come to us in dreams. This story is one of several in this collection that originated from a dream (I'll leave it up to you to guess which ones the others are). In this case, the dream was the first two sentences. The rest was my attempt to put the dream image into some kind of context that would make sense.

It was Dion's turn to sleep with Laura on the last night of the Guard. The rest of us stood sentry outside the bedroom door as per the Protocol, trying not to think of what lay ahead of us in the morning. The dagger that hung from a leather cord around my neck was weighing me down. I saw Travis give his dagger a tug, and wondered if he was feeling the same way. The hover cameras kept a respectful distance, except for the one assigned to me. It had been malfunctioning over the past few days. The fist-sized globe moved through an erratic orbit around my waist. I grabbed it, banged it against the wall a few times, and released it. It wobbled slightly before righting itself, gliding smoothly back into line with the others. For a moment I worried that our overseers would view my assault on the camera as sacrilegious, but luckily its monitor light still glowed a benign green.

Johnny spun his revolver around on his left forefinger. We were each issued with one of the antique firearms at the start, but as far as we knew, the guns weren't loaded, and even if they were, they had probably ceased to function centuries ago. Unlike the daggers, they were mainly for show. The perimeter of the house was guarded for real by a platoon of priestesses, equipped with night vision HUD helmets, automatic plasma rifles and bio-tasers (just in case they only wanted to horribly maim an intruder, as opposed to blasting one into vapour). Still, it made me nervous when Johnny played with his gun.

Travis, who had been a one-pack-a-week man when we entered the Guard thirty-five days ago, was chain-smoking, lighting each cigarette from the dying remains of the last. Thirty-five days. It wasn't a randomly selected number. Five young men, taking turns, each spend a week's worth of nights in the bed of the Offering. Many Ceremonies these days are little more than snuff shows, an excuse for the masses to get off on the gory, protracted deaths of convicted criminals, mentally disturbed masochists and the terminally ill. At some, you even get to vote for the method of dispatch. But not this one. This is the real deal. That's why the five of us agreed to take part.

And, because Laura asked us to. We all went to university together, and all of us loved her, in an unrequited fashion, to some degree. Except for Caleb. It was just lust for him. At least, it was in the beginning. I can honestly say that my love for her had nothing to do with her looks.

I remember the precise moment I fell for her. We were attending a Dedication to Hera as part of our Compulsory Religious Training. Hera's priests had tracked down a small enclave of heretics, devotees of Allah or Jehovah or some such false idol. The audience was nearly rioting with excitement as the captives were herded into the arena, but Laura sat stony-faced and rigid. Moments later the lions entered the ring. Within seconds the largest cat felled a heretic, a pretty young woman about the same age as us. With one swipe of its paw, it disembowelled her. As the girl's screams cut over the roar of the crowd, Laura turned away. Her face contorted for a moment, and a single tear trickled down her flawless cheek. She quickly tried to cover herself, lying feebly about a speck of dirt caught in her eye, but I had seen her true pagan nature, her innate gentleness and compassion. By law I should have marched her straight to the nearest temple for Cleansing, but instead I made a silent vow to protect her, like some beautiful and delicate weed in a garden of Flytraps. How was I to know that my little flower would offer herself up for harvesting?

The Protocol was strict. During daylight hours, we were not permitted to so much as brush against her. There is a commonly held misconception that Aphrodite's Guard consists of a five-week orgy followed by a light slaughter, but it doesn't work that way. It was strictly one-at-a-time, one night after the other, in a pre-set rotation, with precisely three couplings in three different positions each night. That's why only men younger than twenty-two get to participate. We're more likely to be able to fulfil the requirements. The acolytes at Aphrodite's temple gave us a thorough testing beforehand to make sure we were up (pardon the pun) to the job.

The consequences of breaking the Protocol are catastrophic. The last time that happened, Aphrodite rendered the city's entire male populace impotent for six months. The penalty for the Guard members responsible was a corresponding six days of torture, culminating in their death. I think it was the barbed wire gelding that finished them off. On the other hand, the payoff for successfully completing a Guard (besides being allowed to live) is considerable. Women throw themselves at former Guard members, hoping that Aphrodite's blessing will literally rub off on to them. We knew of men well into their forties who were still bedding the most beautiful, wealthy and influential women in the city on the strength of their former service to the Goddess.

Strangely, we never discussed what was in it for Laura. The closest I came to it was on my last night with her, when she asked me what I intended to do after the Ceremony. I answered, then, in a thoughtless moment of post-coital drowsiness, I asked her the same question. She laughed, and said that when she was a little girl she had always wanted to be a goddess. I wish now that I had said what I was thinking, that she didn't have to die to become a goddess – in my eyes, she already was one.

Half an hour before dawn, on the day of her death, Laura and Dion emerged from the bedroom, hand in hand as they were allowed to be until the first rays of sun showed. Laura was already dressed in her ceremonial gown, a translucent white wrap that clung to her body. Dion administered the drug that would relax her, render her compliant, and hopefully, reduce her pain to a pin prick. Although he tried to measure the dose precisely, his hands shook as he poured it out. Her eyes rolled back in her head seconds after swallowing it. She staggered and nearly fell, but Dion caught her. He balanced her on her feet until she could stand unaided, swaying as if she stood on the deck of a ship.

Travis was furious. You idiot, he yelled, what if you've overdosed her? What if the sun comes up, and she can't walk to the summit? Or what if she dies before she gets there? Dion yelled back. I don't care, he said. I'd rather she die of an overdose now, than that I under-dose her and let her suffer. They flew at each other then, and we had to pull them apart. It was the first and only fight any of us had. Then we heard the dawn bells sound from the temple, and it was time to go.

Laura showed no signs of moving, and we were now forbidden to touch her, so we had to prod her in the right direction with a broomstick. It diminished the solemnity of the occasion somewhat. Finally, though, we were all in formation and heading uphill to the sacrificial table some five hundred metres away. The table sat on a plateau, ten paces away from a sheer drop to a rocky beach. Miniature breakers slapped against the rocks. The rising sun dusted the distant whitecaps pink. A stingray-shaped shadow rippled beneath the water's surface and made its unhurried way around a promontory, the distance belying the creature's gigantic proportions. On any other day, the view would have been breathtaking.

A solitary priestess waited for us, anonymous in her magenta hooded robe. No other spectators were permitted. The priestess helped Laura to recline on the table, tethered her at wrist and ankle, and slipped her gown off her shoulders, baring her to the waist. Her nipples stiffened instantly in the cold morning air, and I felt an unwelcome stirring of desire. We stood in single file next to her, Caleb, Travis, me, Johnny, and finally Dion, all of us holding our daggers at the ready.

The priestess nodded. Caleb didn't hesitate. He raised his dagger above his head and plunged it smoothly into Laura's heart. Her eyes widened. She gave a tiny gasp and arched her back in a way obscenely reminiscent of her lovemaking. Travis stepped up next and stabbed her in the chest, and according to the Protocol, the rest of us followed suit. But Caleb's blow had been true – by the time I drove my blade into her, she was already nothing but meat.

It was over in less than a minute. We were all crying, except for Caleb, who walked dry-eyed away from the table and stepped over the edge of the precipice, breaking his neck on the rocks below. Dion laughed hysterically. How's that, Aphrodite, he called to the sky. Two for the price of one! The priestess swung in Dion's direction at his blasphemy, but we were all too deep in our grief to care.

Aphrodite must have decided to overlook his slight, because the ceremony was a resounding success. Birth rates soared, and the temple had to double its recruitment of acolytes to keep up with demand. The tithes it received for the edited highlights of our performances were the highest in holovid history. We were heroes, especially Caleb, who was accorded full honours at his funeral, including the sacrifice of fifteen-year-old twin virgins to accompany him into the afterlife. There's good news for Laura as well. She is getting minor deity status. They've started gathering relics for her shrine, including two locks of hair (one from her head and one from her pubis) and a tiny preserved embryo in a jar, cut from her womb before her body cooled. The priestesses have run DNA tests so that, when Laura's shrine is complete, they can bestow the title of Goddess Consort on the lucky father.

Along with a gold-embossed boxed set of the holovid recordings, we all got our revolvers as souvenirs. Johnny found an aging artisan who crafted a single bullet for each of us to go with them. It turns out that the guns are fully functional after all, because Johnny used his bullet to blow his own brains out. Travis is continuing his service to the Gods. He has volunteered for the annual Tribute to War scheduled for this Sunday. He has been oiling his skin twice a day for a month to make sure it is in peak condition. Only the best human hides will be used to cover the Throne of Ares. Dion is engaged to be married. His fiancée is the only daughter of the wealthiest crime lord in the city. Her money and contacts will come in handy to fuel the prodigious drug habit he has developed recently.

Life hasn't changed much for me, except for one significant detail. Before the Guard I was like any other single man of my age, willing to screw anything that moved, but now I'm just not interested. I tried, Zeus knows I tried, but every time I went to bed with some young lovely I kept picturing Laura's blood spilling out onto the grass. Still, impotence has its compensations. I'm doing much better at school now that I have no distractions - so well, in fact, that if I have the operation, I should be able to apply for a Civil Eunuch position when I graduate. I may have sacrificed my sexuality, but I will not cede my life to the Gods. Someone has to stay to worship at the temple of Laura.

Endangered Species

The mad scientists
and the eco-terrorists
meet one night
to form an unholy alliance.
The *New Zealand Herald*
reports strange phenomena;
Dolphins sprout
adamantine claws
to free themselves
from set nets.
Cats and dogs
limp home at dawn.
They die in pools
of bloodied mucus,
felled by the toxic
breath of kiwi.
The mighty totara
become mightier still,
dissolving chainsaws
in their acid sap.
At the pub,
forestry workers swear
they could hear
the trees laughing.

After the Storm

Kirsten kicked up purple dust as she trudged across the alien plain. The dust irritated her skin, and she scratched absentmindedly at an open sore on her ankle with the long sharpened stick she carried. She stopped for a moment and looked around her, as if she were standing at a crossroads and must decide which direction to take. It was a pointless gesture; except for the occasional squat, fleshy-leaved shrub, the vista was equally featureless no matter which way she looked. She spotted a flurry of movement out of the corner of her eye, and froze as a small furry animal made a break from the cover of a shrub and dashed in front of her. Almost without thinking, she speared it through its side.

The Denvali had a name for the creature, but Kirsten could not pronounce it, so she had called it a pussum. It was mangy and malnourished (much like me, she thought), and its three bulbous eyes rolled in agony as it writhed on the end of her spear and uttered its distinctive breathy squeal. She grimaced as she ended its misery with a quick, savage stomp on its head.

In death, with its eyes sealed shut, it resembled more than ever the pet cat she had as a child on Earth. There was a time when she would have sooner cut off her own arm than harm an innocent being, but it seemed all her principles had been swept away by her instinct to survive. She stooped to stroke its wiry grey fur, then jerked her hand away when she saw the vermin swarming over its body. Suppressing her revulsion, she deftly skinned the pussum, then skewered it end to end on her spear. She stripped the leaves from the branches of a nearby shrub and sucked the moisture from them while she lit a fire and constructed a makeshift spit for her dinner. The creature's flesh charred over the fitful bluish flame.

"Hey!"

Kirsten jumped up and looked around her for the source of the voice, her heart hammering wildly.

"Hey!" A man waved at her, both arms raised over his head as if he were signalling her from a great distance, when in fact he was only thirty-odd metres away. He trotted towards her, a huge grin illuminating his unremarkable face.

"Am I glad to see you!" the man exclaimed. "I was beginning to think I was the only one left alive." He grabbed her right hand and pumped it. "My name's Ben." He smiled intently at her, still shaking her hand, and it took a second or two for her to realise that he was waiting for a response.

"Kirsten," she said. Her voice sounded gruff and strained. She couldn't remember when she last spoke out loud. She looked down at Ben's hand, still holding hers. It was clean, pale skinned and plump. His clothes looked freshly laundered. She pulled her hand away and took a step backward.

Ben glanced from her to the roasting pussum to the plain around them and back to her. "Are you out here on your own, Kirsten? Did any of your people survive?"

"Dead," she said. She squatted to attend to the fire. "All the Denvali are dead."

Ben's smile froze. "I meant the humans in your party," he said.

Kirsten shook her head, partly to answer his question and partly to reprimand herself. She had been criticized more than once by her superiors for becoming too attached to the subjects she observed, and the Denvali's peculiar culture of joyful pacifism had endeared them to her more than any others. She wasn't ready to openly admit to a stranger that she mourned their passing more than that of her colleagues.

Ben nodded in sympathy, misinterpreting her silence for grief. "There were four of us in our bunker," he said. "Samantha got stung by one of those scorpion-mice thingies, Faye got sick–I don't know what from–," his eyes slid sideways, and Kirsten wondered at the reason for the obvious lie, "and Ian just went out one day a week ago and never came back." He gestured toward Kirsten's spit. "Fresh meat," he said. "That must have been a lucky find. What is it?"

She picked up the pussum's bloody pelt on the end of her knife and waved it at him. His face blanched, and his hands fluttered to cover his mouth in an oddly feminine gesture. When he finally lowered his hands, his expression was thoughtful and pitying. "How long have you been living like this?" he asked softly.

Kirsten ran her fingertips over the grooves cut into the handle of her spear. She had started to record the days that had passed since the bomb hit, but had lost heart for the exercise when she passed the fourth month. She shrugged and looked up at Ben.

"Why were you in a bunker?" she said. Her manic blue eyed stare made her seem more animal than human at that moment, tensed ready to spring at his throat if he made a false move.

"Come with me," he said. "I have food – mostly dehydrated or tinned, but it's better than roast alien. I'll fill you in with what I know."

* * *

Ben had a hoverbike. It was designed to be a one-person craft, but Kirsten could just fit if she straddled the battery housing and moulded her body, chest to back and thigh to thigh, against his. He kept up a running commentary as they rode, like a tour guide. His constant stream of chatter, coupled with the strained buzz of the overtaxed engine, had a curiously hypnotic effect on her, and she relaxed into the journey, eyes half-closed, barely registering his words or her surroundings.

"See that round grey patch on the ground? That's a Denvali water sink. There's enough potable water in there to keep five hundred humans alive for two years. Which is lucky for us, because it could take several months for the rescue party to get here," he said. "And over there on the right is where we found our first living thing after the storm – it was a Denvali, but it was too badly injured to survive."

Kirsten tensed. Something in what he had just said unsettled her. Before she could ask him to repeat himself, he braked to a stop, and the moment was lost.

It looked like any other stretch of desert, but Ben took a keypad from his pocket and keyed in a sequence of numbers. A panel slid noiselessly open to reveal a long, well lit flight of stairs. They descended a few steps, and he turned to close the door behind them with another push of a button. Another sequence of numbers opened a door at the bottom of the stairs.

"Welcome to my humble abode," he said, ushering her in with a mock bow.

The room was large and utilitarian. A kitchen took up one wall and four spartan single beds inadequately partitioned from each other clustered against another wall. The rest of the space housed a couple of comfortable looking sofas, a small dining table and a well-stocked bookcase. Ben sung to himself as he pulled a couple of boxes in plain khaki coloured packaging from a kitchen cupboard and threw them into a microwave.

"There's a bathroom through there." Ben nodded towards two doors next to the kitchen. "You're welcome to have a shower, but be warned– the hot water supply is pitiful, so you'll only have ten minutes tops. I'll dig out some of Samantha's clothes for you. You look about the same size."

Kirsten tried the first door. It was locked.

"No, not that one," he said. "That's just a store room." Again, a sideways glance, thought Kirsten. What could he be hiding? She smelt the food as it warmed up in the microwave, and her mouth watered. Perhaps she had been away from human contact for too long, she told herself, and had forgotten how to read people. She shook her head and entered the bathroom.

She emerged ten minutes later, pink-skinned and clad in a dead woman's dress. "Oh, look!" laughed Ben. "There was a woman underneath all that dirt!" He nodded at her left hand, still clutching her bloodied spear. "You can put that down, now," he said. "There's nothing to kill down here."

Kirsten glanced at the spear and smiled apologetically. "I hadn't realised I was still holding it," she said. "It's become part of me." She sat down at the table and laid the spear at her feet.

The meal was a mild chicken korma, surprisingly good for a ration pack dinner (although she had to admit that anything would taste good after what she had been subsisting on). Ben ate slowly, his eyes never leaving Kirsten's face.

"I'm glad I found you," he said.

"You're glad?" she said, swallowing a mouthful of curry. "I thought I was going to die alone on this planet." It was the first time she had confronted this awful truth squarely, and now, safe in the company of a fellow human being, she began to cry. Without a word, Ben pulled her up from her chair, wrapped his arms around her and stroked her hair until her tears subsided.

* * *

Their lovemaking had all the awkwardness one would expect from two people who slept together for reasons other than physical attraction. Afterwards Kirsten laid in the crook of his arm with her head on his chest, luxuriating in the steadiness of his heartbeat.

"What was your job here on Denvalia?" she said.

"You go first," he said, nudging her playfully.

Kirsten frowned. She knew nothing about Ben, beyond his first name. The existence of his underground bunker concerned her; the native sentient species the Denvali lived and slept on the planet surface without any protection at all, and the rest of the human scientific community had taken their cue from them, conceding only to lightweight tents for the sake of comfort. The bunker had been constructed with obvious forethought and secrecy. Yet she sensed that if she tried to press Ben for answers too directly or too soon, she would get nowhere. She sighed.

"I'm a xeno-anthropologist," she said. "I was exploring some underground caves for signs of Denvali relics when the bomb hit. I guess that's what saved my life. Much like your bunker saved yours."

Ben shook his head. "It wasn't a bomb," he said. "It was a storm. An unpredictable, one-in-five-hundred-years storm, the meteorologists said."

Kirsten pushed herself up on her elbow and stared at him. "What meteorologists?" she said. "Everyone's dead! And you're trying to tell me that a storm that destroyed almost everything with nerve endings on the surface of the planet? I'm no meteorologist, but I'm pretty sure the only thing that could do that is an illegal bio-bomb. I don't know who would want to wipe out a harmless species like the Denvali, let alone all the humans who were working here, but…"

"You're right," Ben said. "You're just a bleeding heart anthropologist, so for one thing, you don't know the first thing about extra-terrestrial weather conditions, and secondly, you have no regard for the difficulties involved in sharing a habitable planet with another sentient species – especially one like the Denvali, who have no technological achievements to share with humankind."

Kirsten scrambled backwards in horror off the bed as the implication of his words sunk in.

"Come on, Kirsten," he said. "Denvalia is damn near Earth's identical twin. Hospitable climate – except for those five-hundred-year storms, of course," he chuckled at his own humourless joke, "breathable atmosphere, water, fertile soil…sure, it's pretty barren and boring now, but nothing that a decent sized city or two and a few fast growing pine forests won't fix. We can't let a backward little tribe of humanoids get in the way of colonising the planet."

Kirsten snatched up her spear from the floor and held it in front of her like a talisman. "And the humans you killed?" she said, her voice shaking with rage.

Ben shrugged. "You know what they say – you can't make omelettes without breaking a few eggs. But look on the bright side. You're still alive, and I'm still alive, and we can keep each other company until our ship comes in. What do you say?" He patted the bed next to him as Kirsten inched her way back towards him.

* * *

Kirsten emerged from the bunker into the cool Denvalian dawn. Ben would not have let her live, she told herself. He might have kept her around for his own amusement for a few months, but he could not take the risk of her returning to Earth alive and telling others the truth about what had happened on Denvalia. This was her only course of action.

The Denvali would not have understood. Jealousy, anger, hatred, fear – negative human emotion in general had been beyond their comprehension. Perhaps in some perverse way, Ben had been merciful, bringing them a swift and sudden death rather than the slow degradation they would have faced being overrun by human colonists.

She took a final look down the stairwell at the long, unbroken smear of blood left from dragging Ben's body to the surface. Hefting her freshly stained spear, and with her backpack bulging with pilfered supplies, she set off across the desert, her footprints already wafting away in a gentle morning breeze.

One True Faith

"Did I tell you that I sold my 'Swimming In A Dead Man's Ashes' story to 'That's Life'?" This startling announcement came from Lorraine, a fellow member of Phoenix, the Wellington speculative fiction writers' group to which I belonged. Swimming In A Dead Man's Ashes... what an exquisitely creepy and enigmatic phrase. The resulting story is, pardon the expression, a million miles away from the original true life tale. Thanks, Lorraine, for the inspiration.

Talia shivered at the side of the pool despite the humid heat. The raspy monotone voice of the Shostark irritated her. The planet's emanations had wreaked havoc on his genes; his hairless and earless head, scaly purple-hued skin, and distorted vocal cords suggested that he was one of a handful of humans who were fourth generation Vermanian. She felt faintly ill at the prospect of her descendants looking like that. Not that she intended to have any Vermanian descendants, or any descendants at all, for that matter. Even if she had wanted to, the birth rate on Vermania was so low, even the birth of a mutant like the Shostark was greeted with joy. She switched her attention to the distant sound of the sandstorm battering the surface of the planet somewhere overhead. Seven more months, and she'd turn eighteen. Then she'd be on the next shuttle off this Godforsaken planet and away from these creepy heretics.

The Shostark took a ladle, dipped it into a polished obsidian bowl, and cast its contents over the waters. A coarse grey ash settled on the surface. He murmured a final incantation, and then motioned to the mourners. Aunt Celia and Uncle George, Xavier's parents, were first.

They entered the pool hand in hand, briefly submerged themselves, and then climbed out the other side. Their white robes clung unflatteringly to their bodies and ash stuck in clumps to their face and hair like a virulent skin disease. Aunt Celia stumbled as she stepped away from the pool. Her face contorted with grief as she accepted the Shostark's steadying touch at her elbow.

Talia hung back until she was the last person left to enter the pool. Trembling, she clenched her fists at her sides. Not for the first time, she silently cursed her family's prosperity. If her aunt and uncle hadn't made a fortune mining on Vermania, her parents would not have purchased one of the few remaining licenses and moved here to join them. They wouldn't have been forced to forsake their Earthly religion. Aunt Celia and Uncle George wouldn't have been able to afford the full funeral rites for their son, and right now she would be receiving a ceremonial daubing on her forehead instead of having to bathe in her dead cousin Xavier's ashes.

The water looked muddy from the passage of the mourners before her. Swallowing her revulsion, she descended into the pool and completed the ritual as quickly as she dared. Her skin felt gritty from the remnants of ash coating her. Her wet mourning robes outlined every curve of her body, and she felt a surge of triumph as she noticed several of the male mourners looking at her with unguarded lust.

Xavier used to look at her like that. She had wielded her vow of chastity like a weapon, revelling in his pain as he had reached out to her again and again, only to be rejected every time. She'd even heard whispers that it was her treatment of him that had destroyed his fragile hold on sanity and sent him walking on the surface unprotected in a sandstorm. Her face flushed with anger at the thought, and she ducked her head, tipping her long blonde hair over her face to hide her flaming cheeks. She glanced sideways from behind the curtain of hair to check the Shostark's reaction. He was looking at her too, but his expression was unreadable. She looked away and followed the other female mourners into an antechamber to get dressed.

* * *

Someone is in her room, standing over her bed. Her mouth works as she tries to call for help, but she cannot make a sound. The intruder leans close to her. It is Xavier. He reaches his hands out to her and takes hold of her shoulders. His skin changes on contact with hers, large purple scales forming and spreading up his bare arms like a stain. He flings the bed-clothes aside and tears her nightgown from neck to hem. She opens her mouth again to scream, and it suddenly fills with sand. She is coughing and choking on it, trying to clear it from her throat. It spills onto the floor with a sound like a whisper. Xavier lowers his weight onto her naked body as she fights in vain to draw a breath...

* * *

"Are you feeling alright?" her father said at dinner one night. "You look terrible. And this is the third night in a row that you haven't touched your dinner. You should see a Shostark."

Privately, she had to admit that she felt terrible. After Xavier's funeral, she had defied the ritual proscription against bathing and had washed off the remnants of Xavier's ashes as soon as she had got home, but it felt as if the grit had seeped through her pores and settled under her skin. The nightmares had unsettled her to the point where she was afraid to go to sleep. She felt constantly restless and irritable, and couldn't concentrate on even the simplest task.

"No, thanks. I'd rather go to a real doctor. Oh, except, I forgot," she said sarcastically, "the Shostarks won't let any real doctors step foot on Vermania, much less set up practice. Instead we have to put up with their mumbo jumbo."

Her younger brother Samuel guffawed. "You're so hot for the One True Faith back on Earth," he said, waving his fork at her, "but that's the biggest pack of mumbo jumbo I've ever heard. 'Thou Shalt Not' this and 'Thou Shalt Not' that—and who was the genius who came up with the whole 'burning in hell' idea? I'd take the Shostarks over those lunatics any day."

"You've been on Vermania too long," she said. "The Shostarks have brainwashed you."

"And you have been here too long too," said her mother, "if you have forgotten what it was like on Earth. Poverty, disease, degradation—we're lucky to have escaped it, and we've got the Shostarks to thank for our good fortune."

"The people on Earth suffer because they sin," said Talia. "I won't suffer because I keep myself pure. As soon as I turn eighteen, I'm going back to Earth to train to be a High Priestess, and you can't stop me."

"You're right," her mother said calmly. "I can't stop you once you're eighteen. But right now, you are my responsibility. You will consult a Shostark tomorrow, and that is final."

* * *

The Shostark that attended Talia was so mutated, she couldn't even tell its gender, if it even had one. Its eyelids opened and closed vertically, and its fingers were partially fused together with flexible fleshy webbing which was the only visible part of its body that wasn't covered in dark purple scales.

"Describe your symptoms, please," it said in a flat atonal voice.

She crossed her arms across her chest and leaned back in her chair. "If you Shostarks think you're so good, you should be able to tell just by looking at me," she sneered.

It blinked several times before answering. "Under our care, nobody dies on Vermania except from old age or serious accident. And yet, you don't trust us." It cocked its head to one side. "Why is that?"

Talia snorted. "We've got this stinking planet to thank for that, not you. Nothing can survive here, except for us – if you can call this living. It's like Vermania is hermetically sealed."

The Shostark twisted its scaled face into a smile. "What a perceptive child you are," it said. "Open your mouth, please."

Talia defied its request for several seconds, and then sullenly complied. The Shostark leaned forward and scraped a forefinger around the inside of Talia's mouth before she had time to protest. It sat still and silent, staring unwaveringly at its forefinger for a full minute. Talia squirmed in her chair.

60

Finally it broke from its trance. It slowly lowered its finger and met Talia's gaze.

"Ah," it said.

Even although she professed a lack of faith in Shostark medicine, its air of solemnity unnerved her. "What? What is it? What's wrong with me?"

"There is nothing *wrong* with you," said the Shostark. The hair on Talia's neck prickled at the stress it placed on the word 'wrong'. "When was the last time you had sexual intercourse?"

"How dare you!" Talia spat. "I am a devotee of the One True Faith. I'm only going along with all this Shostark bullshit because my family makes me. I am keeping myself pure so I can become a High Priestess when I return to Earth."

The Shostark smiled again, wider than before, and swayed slightly towards her in a way that reminded her uncomfortably of a cobra about to strike. "I regret to tell you," it said in a tone that suggested anything but regret, "that your path lies elsewhere."

"What are you talking about?"

"You attended a funeral recently, did you not?"

"Yes, but..."

"Your cousin's funeral. Your young, male cousin's funeral."

The crawling sensation under Talia's skin had intensified. Eddies of nausea began to swirl in the pit of her stomach, and she felt the first pulses of a headache that promised to incapacitate her before the afternoon was out. She rose on shaky legs and backed away from the Shostark, her chair clattering to the floor. A small paring knife lay on a side table next to a bowl of fruit, and she snatched it up, unsure of what she would do with it but needing the spurious security it gave her to hold something between herself and the Shostark. "Tell me what is going on," she said, "or so help me..."

"You're pregnant," it said.

The knife slid from her limp fingers. "Impossible," she whispered.

The Shostark shook its head. "The energy of the Universe strikes a delicate balance on Vermania—few die, few are born. But this exquisite balance allows that energy to vibrate strongly. Our most fervent wishes are often granted, and in ways that some might indeed call 'impossible'. Your family craved wealth, and now they have it. Your cousin Xavier's deepest yearning was to join with you, and now he has achieved a more intimate union than he could ever have imagined. And you...you want to be worshipped."

It slid from its seat and knelt at Talia's feet. "And now you carry in your womb the first fully mutated human Vermanian. We cannot tell how far the mutation will go, but we know it will be magnificent. Our wishes, too, have been granted." The Shostark's eyes glittered as it bowed and touched its forehead to Talia's sandaled feet. It rose, and then bowed again, repeating the obeisance over and over, Talia's howls of anguish all but drowning out the accompanying chant.

"Mother..."

An Ill Wind

Sit quietly, he says,
And listen to the wind.
There are no more birds,
So picture instead
Soaring gliders
And microlights,
Those delicate vehicles
Of peace.
I am sorry, teacher.
This is meant to be
Meditative,
But all I can hear
Is the Mistral coming
To strip our bones.

Trading Up

The brief was simple – write a story with the first sentence "Mamma has always had a love for other people's possessions". My first thought on reading the sentence was "what would make for a particularly unusual possession to covet?"

Somewhere between my computer and the editor's desk for the originally intended publication, the submission got lost. But it went on to find another home (twice).

Mamma has always had a love for other people's possessions. Her house is like a giant magpie's nest. Everything in it is second-hand, some items legitimately purchased but most stolen. A collection of knick-knacks clutters her mantelpiece, thrown together with no regard for colour, form or value. A trio of pink plaster kittens, bought from a teenage boy for fifty cents after he had won them at a sideshow shooting gallery, is equally valued with the emerald encrusted Faberge egg she lifted from the drawing room of an exiled Russian heiress. Even her husbands all started out as someone else's.

There is one thing, however, that stands out from her purloined belongings, one thing that she coveted above all others, one thing that has proved more costly to possess than she ever could have imagined.

Me.

When Mamma first saw me, I was little more than mist in a dusty bottle. We glimpsed each other through an open doorway as I peered from my glass prison on a shelf in the back room of a curio shop. It was mutual, familial love at first sight. Something in her unfettered spirit called to me, and I to her. The avaricious old man who owned the shop guarded his stock like a vulture over a scavenged carcass, so, even for a practiced thief like Mamma, it took several return visits before she saw her opportunity. With a swirl of misdirection from her saffron silk scarf, she slipped me into a concealed pocket in her jacket and took me home. Once home, she uncorked the bottle, but she did not know that, without a suitable receptacle for me to enter, I could not leave. She pressed her face to the glass and murmured to me, sometimes pleading with me to come out and play, sometimes singing lullabies, and sometimes uttering nonsensical terms of endearment. Never did she become angry or disheartened. Day by day she sat with me, while her other less cherished belongings gathered dust, her face grew lined and haggard, and her fourth husband left her. She barely noticed, so intense was her infatuation with me.

Two years to the day after she found me, fortune struck. Mamma was carrying her bags into the house after one of her infrequent shopping trips when a sparrow flew in through the open door. It careened in panic about the living room before flying at full speed into a window, dashing its little brains out and falling to the floor. I felt the old familiar pull of the void left by its departing life force. Almost without my volition I slipped out of the neck of my bottle and flowed into the bird's body.

Ah, the freedom! The delirious, intoxicating freedom! For a moment I forgot about Mamma as I flexed my tiny muscles and took to the air. She frowned up at me, not yet aware of what had happened. I landed next to my bottle and pecked at it. She shooed me away angrily. Snatching up the bottle and peering into it, she turned white as she realized it was empty. I fluttered down and landed on her shoulder. She raised her hand as if to dash me off, when she recognized something in my chirruping. Tears of joy filled her eyes as we touched for the first time, her forefinger stroking my head, as delicate as a butterfly kiss.

She called me Jeannie. It was a private joke. Unlike the mythical spirits I was named after, I have no power. I could not smite her enemies. I could not provide her with material wealth. I could not grant her any wishes, save for one, the single wish her starved soul desired – unconditional love.

Trading Up

My new form allowed me scarcely more ability to communicate than my old one, but I was grateful to have the use of all five senses. In time, however, I was no longer able to maintain the sparrow's body. It began to disintegrate around me. I shed feathers at an alarming rate, and soon was unable to fly. Mamma was concerned, then frantic when my skin began to bleed and peel. Pressing her hand to her mouth to stem her sobs, she fled the house. I thought she had abandoned me to my fate, which would be dire indeed. Without a corporeal form, or the correct incantation to send me back into my bottle, I would be cursed to an eternal half-life in the void between heaven and earth. But Mamma soon returned, clutching a plastic bag that sagged with the weight of a freshly gassed cat.

It was a beautiful creature, part Siamese with a glossy pure black coat, but in that body I was a poor substitute for what she really longed for, which was a child of her own. It wasn't long before she devised a solution. She developed a relationship with a local funeral director, and, using a combination of sexual favours and blackmail, she procured the cadaver of a young child. I could not leave the house for fear of being seen by former relatives, but that was no great hardship. I have lived for hundreds of years, so the outside world holds little mystery to me. Far more fascinating was the kindred spirit I had found in Mamma.

But the day soon came when Mamma needed to arrange a new body for me. She went to visit her undertaker friend, only to find the funeral home locked up and vacant. It seemed that bartering bodies for sex was not his only vice, and he had been arrested. She offered to get me another animal body in the interim, but I told her that, having progressed to higher life forms, from bird to cat to human, it was impossible for me to go backwards. I must take another human form.

This was a lie. Although the comparative strength and agility of animal bodies has its compensations, I much prefer humans. For me, there are no substitutes for a functioning voice box and opposable thumbs. Besides, I had Mamma's best interests in mind. I was sure that she would find taking a backward step to animal bodies to be unsatisfactory as well.

For two days Mamma paced about the house chewing her nails and muttering, pausing only to glance nervously in my direction. When I began to slough off rashers of skin, she got desperate. She dressed us both in scarves and dark glasses, bundled me into the back of a Ford Fairlane that had taken her fancy in the supermarket parking lot (it was mainly the fluffy dice she was after) and took to the streets in search of a new body.

What we found was a five-year-old girl, alone in a playground after dark. Beneath her snarled blonde hair, dirty scabbed knees and dull pain-filled eyes, I saw a beauty surpassing any of the forms I had ever occupied. It was obscenely easy to take her. She must have thought she had little to fear from a gentle-voiced woman and another (albeit strangely attired) small child, so she climbed into the car readily on the promise of a hot meal and a ride home.

Her death was peaceful. After dinner Mamma drove around dimly lit streets until the girl fell asleep in the back seat. Using a similar technique to the one she used to dispatch the cat many months ago, she asphyxiated her with noxious gases fed into the car from its own exhaust. As my current body was already technically dead, I was able to sit safely next to the girl and take possession of her body at the precise moment of expiration. I caught a glimpse of her soul as it rushed toward the afterlife with a speed only seen in the very old and the very young. It was mostly coloured in the bright golden glow of joy, but with two distinct dark stripes of resignation and reproach. I did not tell Mamma of this. Even with her fluid notion of morality, taking a young child's life was causing her considerable discomfort. It was better for her to think that the girl went entirely willingly into the afterlife.

I don't know how the police found Mamma. Now she is in jail, and I am in the care of strangers. From what I can ascertain from eavesdropping on my keepers' conversations, the initial charge against Mamma of child abduction could become more serious. They think that I was seriously mistreated in her care, because I have no memory of my life prior to her arrest. I hear terms like "amnesia", "ten year sentence", and "Post Traumatic Stress Disorder". Several doctors have seen me. They have stripped me naked and all but turned me upside down in search of scars, and sure enough, they found them. They are unaware that those scars were inflicted by someone else before Mamma found their daughter. The situation would be laughably ironic, were we not in agony over our separation. And if the doctors were horrified by what they found, just wait until the little girl's body starts to reject the foreign entity inside it.

I calculate I have about two weeks before that process begins. How fortunate that I have a human body now, not an avian or feline one, or my plan would be nigh-on impossible to execute. I will have to obtain a new body for myself. This one may be small and weak, but it can still wield a knife in the dead of night. Then I will exchange a series of bodies, seeking forms of increasing strength and influence, until I find the one that is best equipped to release Mamma. I believe the modern term for this is "trading up".

Something about my intended course of action bothers me. Ah, yes. If I remember correctly, the last time I found myself temporarily without a master, I did something similar. The townsfolk were less than pleased, so they employed a sorcerer of immense knowledge and power to imprison me behind glass. But I need not fear. The old magic has been long since forgotten. There is no one in this world of shysters and charlatans who can stop me.

Don't fret, Mamma. I am coming for you.

Dreamcatcher

Leigh slurped her coffee and waited for the caffeine hit to take effect. She looked at her six year old son Patrick, who slumped at the breakfast table, sporting dark circles under his eyes.

"You had nightmares again last night," she stated. And the night before, she thought, and the night before that. "What were they about?"

Patrick shrugged.

"Don't remember," he lied.

Leigh sighed. "Is it your dad?" she asked.

Again, a shrug.

I know how you feel, mate, she thought. I'm not ready to talk about it myself.

She got up from the table and busied herself in the tiny kitchen of the flat she had rented since her marriage fell apart six months ago. It had been three weeks since they had last heard from Andrew, which was a relief for Leigh but hell on her son.

"You know what I think might help?" she said. "A dreamcatcher."

"Where do you buy dreamcatchers, Mum?"

Thinking on her feet, she said, "They work best if you make them yourself out of things you find in your favourite outdoors place."

Patrick said "Like the beach?"

"Yes–like the beach!"

* * *

Leigh nursed her aging Corolla on the half hour drive to the coast. By mid-day their plastic bags were bulging with scavenged treasures. As soon as they got home, they started on their project, mingling hair and breath as they cut, tied, arranged and glued. Finally Patrick declared the dreamcatcher finished. Leigh leaned back and massaged complaining muscles in her neck. She held up their creation for them both to admire.

It looked as if it had been woven by some drunken mutant spider. The driftwood framework was vaguely circular in shape, and plastered with shells and stones. Thick plastic green twine intersected at haphazard angles with ragged straw-coloured string and almost invisible fishing nylon to form the web. An uneven row of seagull feathers hung from the bottom.

"What do you think?" she asked.

"Cool!" breathed Patrick.

Leigh pinned the dreamcatcher over the head of Patrick's bed. He bit his lower lip as he studied it.

"Mum? How do dreamcatchers work?"

"Umm... well, all the good dreams fly down through the web and in to your head at night, because they're little and light as air." She fluttered her hands over his face and brushed his cheeks with her fingertips, making him giggle. "But the bad dreams are much bigger and heavier, and when they try to come down through the dreamcatcher, they get stuck."

Patrick spread his arms wide and stretched out his fingertips. "I bet we're going to catch a dream this big!"

Leigh was shaken awake early the next morning by a small body leaping up and down on her bed. "Mum, Mum!" Patrick shouted between bounces. "Come and see my dreamcatcher–it worked!" He steered her to his bedroom as she bumped, sleep-blind, down the hallway.

The dreamcatcher sagged on the wall under the weight of several gelatinous blobs. The smallest ones were almost pretty. About the size of a ten-cent piece, they clung to the innermost strands of the catcher like oversized pale grey dewdrops. The largest, a fist-sized amorphous globule the colour of pond scum, squatted in the centre. Two blobs resembling congealed sump oil dangled from the frame. Leigh prodded one, and it slithered down the wall with a moist sucking sound before splattering all over Patrick's pillow.

"Ewwww! Gross!" cried a delighted Patrick. He skipped in circles around her, peppering her with questions while she cleaned up the mess. "Do ya think we'll catch some more tonight? Is that stuff poisonous? What would happen if it fell on my face at night? Can I take that big one to school for Show and Tell?"

Half an hour later, Leigh had stripped and remade the bed and sponged the wall as clean as she could get it (she rubbed at the faint green stain in the wallpaper and prayed that the landlord wouldn't notice), and she had a bag full of nightmares. The dreamcatcher itself looked untouched, the dreams having been grateful to be shaken free from its strands.

Leigh glanced at her watch. "Shit!" she muttered under her breath. Patrick was running late for school. She chivvied him through his morning routine and led him off to school at a trot. He squeaked through the gates seconds before the morning bell, still clutching a piece of toast from his breakfast. Leigh strolled home as she ran through a mental checklist of her day's chores. She opened the door to her flat, took two steps inside, and stopped in her tracks as she slammed in to a wall of stench.

The air was thick with a bouquet of sour milk, human excrement and rotting cabbage. Leigh hunted down the source, her hand clamped over her nose and mouth. She stopped on the threshold of the bathroom, where she had left the bag of dream blobs for later disposal. The dreams had eaten through the plastic and started to corrode the faded lino. A faint green fog rose from the bag.

"Fuck!" She had a job interview in half an hour. There was no way she'd make it in time if she stopped to clean this up–but if she didn't, she could kiss goodbye to the bond on the flat. Chanting a litany of fucks, she found a garden trowel and a metal bowl, scraped up the ooze, and scoured the floor. She opened every window and door in the flat, and then poured the bowl's contents down the toilet.

Six flushes and several prods of the toilet brush later, and the nightmares still clung to the bottom of the toilet bowl. Leigh let loose a 30-second string of her most creative curses, then sighed and trudged off for more cleaning tools. At least the submersion in water had curbed the smell, she thought as she scooped gloved handfuls of muck out of the toilet. She took the dreams outside and buried them in the garden. By then it was noon. She broke a lifetime rule of not drinking before sunset by washing down her peanut butter sandwich lunch with three glasses of cardboard cask wine.

She was nursing a mild hangover when she met Patrick at the school gates that afternoon, and listened to his chatter with only half an ear. They were halfway down their street before she realised that he had gone silent, and his pace had slowed to a dawdle. She followed his gaze to an ill-kempt weatherboard house three doors down from their home. Behind the house's sagging fence lay a Rottweiler. Its massive, scarred head rested on its front paws as its black eyes tracked every movement in the street.

Leigh scooped Patrick's hand up in hers. Every day they went through this. The dog, whose skinhead owners named him Hitler, would wait for the schoolchildren to walk past, and would throw himself, snapping and snarling, against the gate, causing more than a few children to wet themselves in fright. Foreknowledge of the dog's habits didn't lessen the fear, for there was always the possibility that one day the gate would not hold, or that Hitler would succeed in hurling himself over the top. Leigh led Patrick to the opposite side of the street, and Hitler, deprived of his sport, curled back his upper lip in a lazy snarl.

Patrick relaxed as he approached the safety of his own doorstep. He stopped and wrinkled his nose. "Eww, Mum, what's that smell?"

Leigh sniffed the air. Goddammit, she thought, I buried all that shit this morning! She rounded the corner of the flat and drew up with a gasp at the sight of the garden.

A small crater had formed on the spot where she had been digging earlier in the day. The same noxious vapour that had filled the flat rose from the hole. All plant life in a five-foot radius around the hole lay crisp and blackened on bare earth. They tiptoed up to the edge of the hole and looked down. The blobs nestled in the hole, looking unchanged from when they had first appeared.

"What are my dreams doing out here, Mum?" asked Patrick.

"Well, I couldn't keep them inside! They were making a hole in the floor and stinking up the place!"

"But I can't play outside now!" His bottom lip quivered. "I wish Dad was here. *He'd* know how to get rid of them properly." He stomped off in to the flat in a sulk. Leigh stared at the hole in the ground, her eyes pricking with the sting of his words.

* * *

Patrick's dreamcatcher was dripping with dream blobs again the next morning. Leigh shook them into a bowl.

"It's OK," she assured him. "Today is rubbish day. I'll get rid of them all." She had no idea what she was going to do for the next seven days, though.

Leigh triple-bagged two nights' worth of dreams and lugged them out to the street, her muscles trembling with the effort as she held them at arm's length in front of her. Patrick trotted beside her, his school bag on his back. The rubbish truck pulled up level with them as she dropped her bundle in the gutter. It slapped like a butchered carcase against the tar seal.

The rubbish collector, a tattooed man mountain in a torn T-shirt and running shorts, frowned at Leigh. "You got nightmares in there?" he demanded, jerking his head at the bulging bag.

"Uh…yeah. Is there a problem with that?"

The man shook his head. "You can't put nightmares out in the rubbish."

She crossed her arms tightly across her chest. "I checked with the council. They didn't say anything about nightmares being not allowed."

"Sure," replied the collector, "you're *allowed* to put them out for collection–but there's no point. They'll only come back, twice as bad."

"Well, how am I supposed to get rid of the damn things?"

The rubbish collector exchanged glances with the truck driver, who was leaning out of the window of the truck. The driver raised his eyebrows a millimetre, leant back inside the cab, and turned up the radio. Strains of "Californication" filled the air. The collector slowed his speech to half-speed, as if addressing a moron. "You have to send them back to whoever gave them to you."

"What…what do you mean?"

The collector rolled his eyes and tapped his size 13 foot. "Look. Whose dreams are they?"

Leigh nodded at Patrick. The collector squatted down and addressed him man-to-man.

"Here's what you gotta do, mate. You gotta figure out who's scaring you, or stressing you out. Then you gotta match the dream shapes to the person, package them up and send 'em back."

The collector glanced at Leigh, then hunched closer to Patrick, mumbling in his ear so Leigh couldn't make out the words. Patrick nodded, wide-eyed. The collector drew back and straightened. "Then the dreams will stop, and there you go–problem solved."

"Alright then, love?" he said to Leigh, patting her on the shoulder and sending her staggering backwards. He jogged off down the road. They stood in the street and watched him heft rubbish sacks and wheelie bins until he was the size of an action figure against the horizon.

* * *

Leigh woke Patrick shortly before dawn. Silently, she covered the kitchen floor with a plastic sheet, while Patrick concentrated on lighting the dozens of tea light candles she had arranged along the bench. She placed three nights' worth of dreams in metal bowls on the floor, their stink muted under water.

Leigh consulted her list. "Mrs Worthington-Smythe," she announced. Mrs Worthington-Smythe was the substitute teacher Patrick had had since his regular teacher had gone on maternity leave. She was two years away from retirement, and yearned for the days when she was legally entitled to beat her young charges with leather straps. These days she had to limit herself to meting out verbal thrashings.

Patrick perused the selection of nightmares before him, and pointed out three lumpy lavender coloured blobs. Leigh wrapped them in tinfoil, and then tissue paper, lowered them in to a glittery gift box, and tied it shut with a large red velvet bow. With a flourish, she drew a black line through her name on the list, and moved to the next one.

"Bradley Knox." Bradley was a much older, much larger boy at Patrick's school. He spent his lunchtimes sitting on the top of the jungle gym and prising open the fingers of other children. Patrick had so far flown below Bradley's radar, but he lived in dread of the day when Bradley realised he existed. Patrick selected a large, spongy-looking slime green globule. Leigh packaged it in a shoebox and covered it in Spiderman wrapping paper.

"Hitler." Patrick indicated an assortment of ragged-edged fleshy lumps. Leigh concealed them inside two pieces of schnitzel tied up with twine.

"Uncle Jacob." Patrick loved his fifteen year old uncle Jacob, even although he had still to get over his fear of the dark since Jacob had told him about monsters under his bed. Leigh took the fluorescent yellow globs Patrick had picked out and shut them in an old video case.

Leigh took a deep breath. "Dad." Patrick chose one glistening midnight black globe, and wrapped it himself, shakily addressing the hand-decorated packaging with a green Vivid marker.

Patrick divided the remaining dreams into two piles. One motley assortment of blobs Leigh put in an empty ice cream container ready to drop off at the local video store. There was the repository of all the scary movies Patrick would have been better off not watching. The other pile held the little grey dewdrops. He lingered longest over these ones. He cradled them in a small cane basket, wrapped the basket in cellophane, and then put the package in to a larger box, which he decorated in dozens of hand-drawn red hearts. He bent low over the box as he addressed it, blocking Leigh's view.

The dreams seemed to know that they were on their way home. They sat, inert, in their packaging. They blew out the candles in time to see the first rays of sun filter through the curtains. When it was time to leave for school, Leigh gathered up the dreams in a large cardboard box, ready for distribution.

First stop was Hitler. Leigh threw the schnitzel package over the fence. The dog leapt up and caught it in mid-air, swallowing it in two gulps. He shook his head, flicking ropes of saliva from his jaws, turned around twice, and then settled back down in the sun for his morning nap.

Once at school, Leigh slipped in to Patrick's classroom. She checked that she was unobserved before leaving the red-ribboned box on Mrs Worthington-Smythe's desk. Then she kept guard while Patrick snuck in to Bradley Knox's classroom. Mission accomplished, they exchanged grins and high fives.

Leigh took her remaining parcels to the local shopping mall. She slid the ice cream container in the after-hours returns slot at the video store, posted the others, and then headed for home. She slowed as she approached Hitler's house. The dog lay sleeping in his customary spot. His back legs twitched and jerked, and he whined softly, caught in the throes of a doggy dream. When Leigh and Patrick drew level with Hitler's gate that afternoon after school the dog started up as usual as if to lunge at them, but then seemed to change his mind, dropping his hindquarters to the ground and whimpering before running out of sight behind the house.

Patrick's dreamcatcher was empty the next morning. He raced to school with unusual enthusiasm, and was equally eager to tell Leigh about his day on his way home.

"Bradley Knox wasn't there today, Mum. I think he was sick. And Mrs Worthington-Smythe was sick, too. She was at school in the morning, but she had to go home after lunch, and our class had to squash in with Room 3. She must have been hurting really bad, because she was crying, and I heard Mrs Huntley tell Mr Connor that she didn't think she'd be coming back. I hope we get a nice new teacher instead."

Leigh cleared her mailbox while Patrick raced ahead. She tucked a small heart-covered parcel addressed to her under her arm while she leafed through the junk mail and bills. When she got inside, Patrick was on the phone. Leigh left him to his conversation and went to her bedroom. She opened her parcel and took out the cellophane-wrapped basket inside the box. She peeled off the cellophane and studied the pearly grey globules inside. She touched one, and the surface gave slightly under her fingertips, its colour fluctuating like a quicksilver rainbow. She slid the basket under her bed and rejoined Patrick. He was speaking in monosyllables, his face expressionless.

"Who was that?" she asked when he had hung up.

"Dad." He skirted past her as he headed for his afternoon forage in the kitchen. He walked gingerly, as if he were nursing a deep-seated pain.

"Well–what did he say?"

"Not much." Patrick dipped a biscuit in a glass of milk. "He hasn't been to see me because he's been busy getting ready for a new job. It's in Australia."

Patrick brightened as he continued. "He said he'll be making heaps more money, so I'll be able to visit him there in the holidays. And he said he's going to take me to Seaworld!"

"Will you miss him?" she asked.

He thought about this for a moment. "I dunno…will you?"

"No."

He planted a crumb-studded kiss on her cheek. "Then neither will I."

* * *

Leigh dreamed that night. A squad of faceless men pursued her through a forest. She tried to run, but it was like wading through chest deep water. She scuffed through a carpet of decaying pine needles. Two men caught her by the arms, and a third levelled a gun to her head. They forced her to her knees. She could see Patrick, several metres away, screaming in terror and reaching out for her as another man clutched him up. Her dream logic told her that they would not harm him. Orphan him, yes, but not harm him.

"Don't let him see!" she yelled. "Kill me if you have to, but don't let him see! Don't let him see…"

Leigh woke herself with her own tears. She sobbed in the dark until the pain of the nightmare subsided. She reached for the light switch and hung her head over the side of the bed. From her upside down perspective she could see that the cane basket was empty.

She padded in to Patrick's room. His dreamcatcher still hung unfilled above his head. He was deep in sleep, with one foot dangling over the edge of his bed and both fists bunched up under his chin. She edged in to the bed next to him and enfolded him in her arms. He made a soft protesting sound, and then settled in to her embrace. She breathed in the green apple scent of his hair until she reclaimed her own dreamless sleep.

Pierced

Grandpa mutters,
There's mysterious goings-on next door.
He doesn't understand
the neighbour's
electric-blue hair,
death-black lips,
metal-skewered flesh;
one man's beauty
is another's
mutilation.
He tires of listening
to her screams,
sound swirling
beyond
the bounds
of concrete walls.
A door opens,
a skull splits,
instead of blood,
Light flows.

Lapp Dancing

Every year, the Phoenix writers' group sets itself a Christmas theme to write to. Participation is optional, but highly encouraged. The year I wrote "Lapp Dancing", the theme was "Tragedy at the North Pole".

Sometimes you just have to forget about the lofty themes and the meaningful commentary on the human condition, and write things just for fun. This was one of those times.

I needed to disappear for a while. Luckily Sneaky Pete owed me a favour, and he's the best "disappearer" in the business, which is how I ended up working for Layla, an anorexic chain-smoking dwarf with a penchant for wearing green. She owned a bar in Lapland, where I was to spend part of an Arctic winter pulling pints and fending off advances from drunken Finnish lumberjacks.

I'd just got word from Pete that it was safe for me to go home. A few more weeks at Layla's, and I'd have enough money for my airfare. It was a quiet night in the bar, and I was fantasizing about barbeques at the beach, margaritas by the pool and tanned men in shorts, when in he walked.

He seemed to fill the doorway, blocking the wind with his bulk as he stamped the snow off his massive black boots. He looked up, and a tremor ran through the dozen or so drinkers in the bar. Must be some kind of local celebrity, I thought, as patrons raised their glasses in unsteady hands and toasted the newcomer.

Layla beckoned him over from the top of her bar stool with the built-in stepladder, where she was holding court with assorted paper mill magnates and reindeer herders. Standing on tiptoe, she was just able to kiss his chin. "Nick, darling!" she said. "How lovely to see you!" She snapped her fingers in my direction. "Amber, make sure you look after Nick. All drinks on the house."

Nick took a stool at the bar. His lush white beard and fleshy cheeks obscured a face that looked as though it would customarily be twinkly-eyed and smiling. No smiles tonight, though. He slumped in his seat, his beard brushing the counter. "Bourbon," he said. I tried not to slop his drink on the floor as I stared, transfixed, at his hands. They were huge, fat and white, like a pair of pillows tacked on the end of his arms. There wasn't a callous in sight. Obviously not a lumberjack, then. He downed the bourbon in one gulp, signalling for another before his glass left his mouth.

"Women trouble?" I guessed. He looked startled and nodded. "Don't tell me," I said as I pushed his glass towards him, "your wife doesn't understand you, right?"

"Worse," he replied. "She doesn't believe in me anymore."

"I don't get it," I said.

"It's those bloody Jehovah's Witnesses," he said, as if talking to himself. "If they hadn't knocked on our door, we'd still be a happy couple. Coming into my house, filling her head with nonsense, converting her...if I get my hands on them, I'll..." He trailed off, his face contorted with rage and his fists clenched. Suddenly his hands looked considerably less pillow-like.

I still didn't get it, but then, I'm a barmaid, not a psychiatrist (although customers frequently get the two confused). I poured him another bourbon. "Perhaps you should go home and talk to her," I said. "You're not going to make things any better by sitting here."

He nodded. "You're right," he said. "That's exactly what I'm going to do." He knocked back his drink, slammed the glass down on the bar and strode off. There was a lull in the wind that was roaring outside, and in the momentary quiet I thought I heard the tinkling of small bells. I felt quite pleased with myself, despite the fact that I'd lost Layla a customer for the night. It wasn't often any of the punters actually listened to me.

He was back the next night, however, looking more morose than before.

"That little talk with your wife didn't go so well, I take it?"

"No, it didn't. And now I've got even bigger problems. Half my staff has come down with cervine flu. At my busiest time of year, too."

"What line of business are you in?" I asked.

"Toys," he replied.

"Really?" I said. "I thought that sort of stuff all came out of sweat-shops in China these days."

"Don't get me started!" he roared, thumping his fist on the bar. Here comes that temper again, I thought, taking a couple of steps backward. "All the cheap plastic crap they turn out...that junk doesn't even make it from one Christmas to the next most of the time."

I could almost see the thunderclouds forming over his head, when he suddenly brightened. "Mind you, you've just given me a good idea," he said. "I could make a few phone calls, pull a few strings, maybe get a couple of Asian factories to switch over to my product line for a week or two..." He gave me a wide-faced smile, the first I'd seen from him, leant over the bar and kissed me full on the lips.

"You're a genius!" he said, and once again he swept off into the night.

I didn't see him again until the night before I was due to fly out. Layla had already turned in, and I was finishing up as my last customer stag-gered out the door. Nick pushed past the exiting lumberjack and all but collapsed at the bar, burying his head in his arms. His shoulders heaved with huge gut-wrenching sobs. Without a word, I lined up three bour-bons. When he had composed himself sufficiently to drink two of them, I dared to ask.

"What's happened?"

"It's Rudolph," he said. "He's dead!"

Who the hell is Rudolph, I thought. His brother? His best friend? His dog?

Nick continued. "He broke his leg this morning. I had to....to shoot him!"

That ruled out my first two guesses.

He fell into another crying fit, then sculled the last bourbon. "I just don't know what I'm going to do without him!" he cried. "I'll never find another lead reindeer in time."

What could I do? I was fresh out of good advice. I came out from behind the bar and gave him a few tentative consoling pats on the shoulder. It only seemed to make things worse. His wailing intensified, and he threw himself into my arms, almost knocking me off my feet. And that's how we stayed for the next half hour, until his tears were spent.

* * *

I'd like to say that I slept with him against my better judgment, but I don't think I have a better judgment. It's not that he was completely unattractive. In fact, he had a strangely powerful allure. Every time I was around him, I felt an almost uncontrollable urge to climb into his lap. One night embracing that mountain of white flab, however, and I was completely over it.

I tried to break it to him as gently as I could. "Look," I said, "There's no future for us. I'm flying home tomorrow. Besides, you're a married man. I make it a rule not to steal other women's men. I just borrow them for a while."

He didn't take it well. "You can't leave me now!" he ranted. "Not after all we've been through together! I need you! Tomorrow's the most important night of the year for me! I can't get through it without you!" By now he was storming around my room, which was essentially a storage room at the back of the bar with a double bed in the corner, and he was breaking stuff with his flailing arms. A forty ounce bottle of rum tumbled from the top shelf and shattered at my feet, closely followed by a bottle of cognac.

I squealed and jumped up on the bed. Nick paused in his rampage, and his eyes narrowed as a malevolent thought entered his head. He picked up another bottle of spirits and, holding it high above his head, hurled it at the floor, where it exploded in a splatter of booze and glass. The ceiling echoed with loud thuds as Layla thumped on the floor of her apartment above us. "What's going on down there?" she yelled.

"Nothing, Layla," I yelled back. "I've got it under control." I turned back to Nick.

"That's it!" I hissed. "Layla's going to take the damage out of my wages. If you don't leave right now, I'm going to call the cops." I waved my cell phone at him to show that I meant it.

"Go ahead!" he said, gesturing widely and destroying another bottle in the process. "I'm highly respected around here. They won't do a thing."

I rolled my eyes and started dialling. Rock stars, politicians, adult movie directors, I've heard them all say the same thing. Nine times out of ten, they learn the hard way that they're not above the law. I hardly thought a local toy manufacturer was going to have much pull.

The two cops that arrived five minutes later were a twin drool fest, with their white-blond buzz cuts, classic Nordic features and chiselled pecs straining against their shirts. I half-expected them to be carrying a portable CD player and wearing tear-away pants. Damn it, I thought, why couldn't there have been a bar brawl that needed breaking up six weeks' ago?

Nick stared intently at one of the cops. "I know you," he said. "Marko Vatanen, isn't it?"

"That's right, said the cop. "I'm surprised you remember me. I didn't get too many visits from you when I was a kid."

"What did you expect?" said Nick. "Pulling wings off flies, stealing money from your mother's wallet, blowing up your neighbour's letterbox with a homemade pipe bomb. . . " Nick counted off the offenses on his overstuffed fingers. "Frankly, I'm astounded you were accepted into the police force."

Marko shrugged. "Are you familiar with the term 'good cop, bad cop'?" he said. "They had a shortage of bad cops." He twisted Nick's arms savagely behind his back and snapped on handcuffs.

"Hang on a minute, Marko," said the other cop. "Aren't you being a bit hasty here? Christmas Eve is tomorrow night. I'm sure this can all be sorted out without having to take him in."

Marko shook his head. "The law's the law," he said gleefully. He marched Nick out the door. His partner trailed after them. I was too intent on cleaning up the mess to give much thought to his parting words.

"But Marko," he said, "think of the kids. . . "

* * *

The first thing I did when I stepped off the plane on Christmas Eve was buy several bottles of fake tan and the skimpiest summer dress I could find. The second thing I did was select a table in a garden bar within stumbling distance of my flat, and order a big creamy cocktail, complete with a little paper umbrella, half a tropical jungle of fruit garnishes and one of those chewy green cherries that nobody likes. The third thing I did was order another one. I can't remember the fourth, fifth and sixth things I did. At some point I must have made my way home, because I woke up the next morning in my own bed with the mother, father, uncle and second-cousin-once-removed of all hangovers. It took me a few seconds to realize that the pounding I could hear wasn't just in my head. Someone was hammering on my door.

It was Sneaky Pete. "Merry Christmas," he said, blowing me air kisses and sweeping into the room. "Oh, good, you haven't unpacked yet." He grabbed me by the arm and propelled me towards the door, scooping up suitcases as he went. "You can dress in the car," he said. "You're in trouble. Again."

"But I've only been back 24 hours," I protested. "That would be a record, even for me."

"It's the Finns," he explained. "You slept with the wrong man. Again. Layla rang me last night. His wife has friends in high places, apparently, and when she found out you'd bedded her husband and had him arrested, she made a few calls and hired Joey the Snake to pay you a little visit."

I shook my head, trying to prompt my few functioning brain cells into some kind of activity. "But... but he said that his wife was some kind of religious convert. That doesn't sound like very pious behaviour."

Pete gave me a pitying look. "Oh, honey," he said, "You didn't fall for the old 'my wife doesn't believe in me' line, did you? Again? Come on. I've got you booked on a flight to Kazakhstan. I've got a contact there who owns a strip club. You'll be safe there – well, safe-ish – until I can sort this out."

I groaned. "Not again!" I followed him to his car. As I stood blinking in the early morning light, I could hear all up and down the street the ear-aching screech of children crying.

Fairy Gothic

This story was inspired by a series of photos of my daughters in fairy costumes. It's short and sweet, just like my girls.

Look at how short their hair is in this first photo. Anna must be about three, which would make Zoe eighteen months old. I think I hired those costumes for Halloween. There's a video of them somewhere, dancing around in these costumes on their chubby little toddler legs. Zoe wouldn't even have known what fairies were back then, she just would have been drawn to the shiny fabric and sequins and tulle. But I think I've managed to capture the "fairy spirit" in this shot.

They've graduated to their own fairy dresses in this photo. You can tell they've dressed themselves. The velcro is fastened all crooked, they've got their favourite T shirts underneath the dresses, and their hair is all over the place. I probably made them put the T shirts on. Back then, they would have run around all day in their undies even in winter, like little urban savages, if I'd let them. This is probably my favourite shot. It's so candid, so unposed, and I love the way Anna has her head resting on Zoe's shoulder. They were always close like that.

How old would they have been in these next ones…eight and nine, maybe? Those fairy dresses are little more than rags in these photos. That's partly why Anna's augmented her outfit with leopard print tights, and Zoe's wearing pink track pants under hers. I think they took these photos of each other—that's why the top of Anna's head is cut off. They're just taking the piss now, taking turns at tying up their dollies and pointing a toy gun at their heads. It would have been Anna's idea; she was always the practical joker. I call it their Guerrilla Fairy phase.

I remember thinking when I first saw these shots that they must have been growing out of being fairies. But no. It turns out that you never grow out of being fairies.

This one was taken before a dance recital. That's why they're wearing makeup, and the costumes are more elaborate. I think it was the year before Anna started high school, so, yes, they were too young for makeup. But you know what these dance school productions are like. And of course, they didn't think they were too young for makeup! It's a little disturbing, this photo, even although they looked so beautiful. Or perhaps it's disturbing because they looked so beautiful, in a conventional, almost sexual way. Those pouting lips, those knowing glances, the way Anna's thrusting out her non-existent breasts... all the fairy spirit seems to have leached out of them, and left just the shiny, glittery shell.

What would you call this one? Fairy Gothic? They made these costumes—it was another Halloween party, I think. It was a bitch trying to track down the right kind of fabric to make those wings. We ended up buying several lengths of muslin and dying it black. They made them so big, they had to spend all night going through doorways sideways, and the black dye rubbed off on everything. They just laughed and said it was fairy dust. At first glance, it might look poles apart from the first photo, but I think it's quite similar. In the first one, their lives had just begun, and in his one, they're on the brink of womanhood. There's that same sense of unfettered possibilities stretching out in front of them. And they've well and truly regained the fairy spirit; if you look closely, you can see that their feet aren't quite touching the ground.

I don't know why I kept this last one. Stupid cheap digital camera—by the time the shutter clicked, they had flown out of frame, and all I got was a blurry shot of their star-clad feet.

Theft of A Servant

Serena leant against the railing of the mezzanine floor, overseeing the latest Collection. The Powers That Be had specified fifty girls between the ages of eight and ten. Serena could only guess at why the girls in this Collection all had to be fair-haired and overweight. They formed docile lines, clutching each other's podgy little arms and chattering excitedly at the prospect of what delights might await them beyond the vault-like doors that bisected the hall.

Serena scowled as she spotted her 2-I-C, Mark Jordan, skirting the edges of the hall. He fluttered around the children in his purple lab coat like some gaudy mutated insect, paused to talk to one of the security guards, then sidled off to engage Kate Gibson. A tall, painfully thin woman of indeterminate years, Kate looked as if she had been stretched and squeezed until all the colour and personality had leached out of her. She was a Mouthpiece for The Powers, which was why Mark spent more time trying to curry her favour than doing any actual work.

Her scowl deepened as she saw a child much smaller than the others join the queue. She looked to be little more than two years old, her dark hair forming a nimbus about her head. Serena stomped down the stairs and yelled at the nearest guards.

"How the hell did she get in here? Does she look like a fat blonde ten-year-old to you? The Collection parameters were quite specific..."

The child turned towards her. Serena's stomach lurched, and her words dried up in her throat. It was her daughter Lexi. Serena caught a glimpse of her dilated pupils in her wide brown eyes before Lexi slowly raised her thumb to her mouth and turned away again without recognition.

Kate glided over to Serena, Mark close on her heels, and interposed herself between Serena and Lexi. Several guards moved to form a phalanx around the women. Kate's eyes rolled back in her head and her mouth fell slackly open. The voices of The Powers issued from her as if she were a human amplifier, making her entire body tremble.

"Three years ago today you finalised the Collection of a group of young men," the voices said. "It was a very small, very select group. Do you remember, Serena?"

How could she forget? It had been a difficult assignment to fulfil. There were only five men in the city who met the requirements; aged between 18 and 22, over 1.7 metres tall, with an IQ exceeding 130, a proven record of superior athletic ability and an above average score on the Universal Indicators of Beauty test.

When she finally had them all rounded up and stood face-to-face with them, she was almost overwhelmed by their beauty. The immediate employees of The Powers were social pariahs, and the pickings in the heavily guarded enclave she was forced to live in were decidedly slim. If that didn't present challenges to her sex life, her own indifferent genetic inheritance certainly did.

She figured The Powers owed her. So, too, did her best friend Bronwyn, a middle-aged woman with bad teeth and worse skin, who was the Collection Centre's chemist. Instead of administering a straightforward sedative, Bronwyn shot them full of a complex psychotropic cocktail of drugs, crafted to maximise suggestibility and compliance, with a hefty dose of aphrodisiacs and a nifty little amnesiac kicker on the comedown. Serena detained the group for an extra twelve hours before sending them to The Powers, and the two women took full, exhausting, ecstatic advantage of their doped-up charges.

And nine months later, Lexi was born.

"We know who your child's father is," said The Voices. "He belonged to us – all of him. Every last fingernail scraping, every last strand of hair, every last drop of blood and bodily fluids. We are reclaiming what is ours."

Before she could move or make a sound, the guards were on her, one to each side and a third behind her clamping a leather-clad hand over her mouth. The last thing she saw as Mark plunged a hypodermic needle into her arm was a towheaded girl taking her daughter's hand and leading her through the doors.

Contact

Once,
the idea of sex with aliens
might have appealed.
But,
having encountered
your loathsome race,
I am cured
of my deviancy.
You,
with your putrid salty stench,
your pore-pitted skin
oozing at the mere
mention of heat.
You,
with appendages
upon appendages
dangling from your
spongy carapace.
You,
with your tiny globular eyes,
your chaotic, misfiring brain,
and that blind pink parasite
squirming inside your mouth.
It's enough to turn
all three
of my stomachs.

On The Border

I was privileged to attend a presentation by Russell Kirkpatrick at Conspiracy II, the New Zealand national science fiction convention in Wellington in 2007. Russell is, amongst other things, a map geek, and his presentation focussed on the use of maps in fantasy novels.

One of the topics he touched on in his fascinating talk was the power of maps to be used as a Force for Evil. Maps are often used as tools of war. And maps can be selective in the truth they present.

So what might happen if the map had its own agenda?

Although he had only been in service to the Book for three years, the Bearer had already forgotten his own name. He had studied the maps inside it so thoroughly the images were seared into his mind, yet he could not say which of them represented his place of birth, nor could he recall the family from whom he had been taken.

An iron chain pierced the bottom corner of the Book and encircled his neck. He dared not let it dangle for fear of crippling himself, so he clasped it tightly to his chest. He shuffled forward as if blinded, and in a way, he was. The constant presence of the Book had skewed his perceptions. The contours of the land showed themselves to him in surreal, giddying colours, and at distances ten times further than any other mortal. But he could no longer see the sky or the stars, and anything else he perceived as little more than a blur. People stood all around him, he knew. He could hear the unsettled murmuring of many voices, and, turning his head, saw the indistinct columns of light that represented living beings; thousands of them, gathered on either side of a half-mile wide strip of sand that glowed a vicious shade of vermillion that only he could see.

"This way, Bearer," came a man's voice at his shoulder. He turned toward it and followed the gesturing figure. His boots dragged through the sand, and he stumbled to his knees. His guide dared not touch him–only he could bear the burden of the Book–so he laboriously pushed himself back onto his feet, swaying slightly in the mid-morning heat. The guide directed him to a small tent, and, holding back the flap, ushered him inside before leaving him alone. Inside the protection of the tent's hide walls, his eyesight returned to something approximating normal. The tent was furnished with a long table on which sat a full inkwell and quill, and a single chair. He sank into the chair, placed the book on the table before him, and waited.

* * *

From their respective sides, the leaders of the two armies watched the Bearer enter the tent. They rode their horses to the front of their lines, dismounted, and approached each other with ceremonial slowness. They stood facing each other for a few moments, their faces impassive, then turned in unison and strode shoulder-to-shoulder to the tent. For one to enter behind the other would suggest defeat, so they entered together, if somewhat awkwardly.

The leader from the North lifted off his helmet, stripped off his gauntlets, and ran his hands through his shaggy white-blond hair, his metal breastplates clanking with every movement. The leader from the South, whose only bodily protection besides her leather battle-dress was the talismanic tattoos on her broad brown cheeks, flashed a vulpine smile.

"Comrade," said the man.

"Brother," said the woman.

They completed their greeting, pressing their right palms and forearms together in the manner of the North, and then pressing their foreheads and noses together in the manner of the South. Although their professional instincts returned their hands close to their weapons, they drew apart and gazed on each other with an expression approaching fondness.

"It would be a great tragedy to see the blood of so many fine warriors shed needlessly here today," said the man.

"Indeed," said the woman. "Although the losses would undoubtedly be greater on your side than on mine."

The man scowled, his jaw tightening, then abruptly laughed, shaking his head. "You have not changed, Maeve."

"But you have, Sacha," she said. "You've become harder to bait."

They both turned their attention to the Bearer. He was a slightly built young man, barely past his twentieth year, Maeve guessed, although his position had prematurely aged him, thinning his light brown hair, carving deep lines of strain on his face, and lending a tremor to his hands that should only belong to a man in his dotage. His eyes flitted about the tent as he struggled to focus. Were it not for the Book around his neck, she would have thought him a half-wit. She swallowed her distaste.

"Open it," she said. "Show us the Borderlands."

He complied, his hands suddenly deft as he found the correct page. Maeve and Sacha bent over the Book. It showed an aerial view of a five hundred square mile area straddling the border between their respective homelands and stretching from one coast to the other. On the western edge, the map featured a miniature of the Cerulean Cliffs, their distinctive blue colouring replicated perfectly. Near the northern edge, it depicted the Aromatic Forest in shades of lush green and autumnal brown, the scent of wood spice seeming to waft up from the page. A thin blue line representing the Yacto River snaked through the forest and across the page to the Eastern border where it widened as it entered the sea. Tiny drawings of houses clustered along either side of the river to show human settlements.

"I never thought it would be so beautiful," said Maeve. Her words suggested appreciation, but her nostrils flared and she leant back slightly as if in the presence of something offensive.

"Yes..." breathed Sacha. "So beautiful..." His eyes took on an unhealthy sheen, and his hand hovered over the page, drawing ever nearer to it.

"No!" the Bearer shouted. Quick as a snake, he smacked Sacha's hand away. Sacha shook himself like a dog and took three deep, shuddering breaths. His bewildered expression gave way to one of fury, and he drew back a fist to strike the smaller man.

"Only I may touch the Book," the Bearer said hastily. "It means certain death for anyone else to lay hands on it. But it will try to draw you in. It yearns for your life force."

Sacha looked at the Book and edged away, drawing his hands in to his chest and rubbing them together as if to reassure himself that they were still attached to his body. Maeve growled deep in her throat. "Then we had best get this over with quickly," she said. She made stabbing motions at the Book with her forefinger. "My sovereign has sent me to take possession of the port here and the farmland to the south of it. We are prepared to go to battle over it if need be, but as you can see by the presence of the Bearer, we believe we can come to a compromise that will be mutually acceptable and that will save many lives."

The Bearer gave a short, barking laugh and shook his head, making the chain around his neck rattle. "Fools!" he said. "There is no bloodless way to carve up the land. The Book will not allow it. The Book..."

The touch of Maeve's blade against the back of his neck silenced him. "If you don't shut up," she said through gritted teeth, "yours will be the first blood the Book will taste today." The Bearer remained quiet. Maeve withdrew her sword.

"In return," she said, turning back to Sacha, "we will cede to you full possession of the Aromatic Forest, this stretch of coastline from here to here, and the Kamankayan plains immediately inland."

"The plains?" asked Sacha softly.

Maeve coughed into her fist. "Yes. The herds of wild horses that roam there are famous for their speed and agility, and we all know how much your queen values good horseflesh."

"But those plains are your birthplace, Maeve. Surely he is not asking you to hand them over."

She shrugged. "Do I look like a sentimental fool to you?" Her tone was light enough, but she turned away from him for a moment. When she turned back, she had composed her face into an impassive mask.

"Do we have an agreement, or not?"

"Almost. I also want this village included in our territories." Sacha indicated a symbol on the map that was little more than a smudge.

Maeve frowned. "Am I missing something? It has no strategic or economic value that I can see."

"No, but it seems that one of us is a sentimental fool."

Maeve's frown deepened with incomprehension.

"I fell in love there once."

Maeve formed a silent "oh", and suppressed a smirk. "It's yours. Bearer, you may formalize our accord. Make the marks."

The Bearer's tremble intensified, until Maeve feared he would collapse into a fit. "Do you know what you are asking me to do?" he said. "There will be consequences. The Book will demand it."

Maeve bent down and whispered in his ear like a lover, her knuckles whitening around her sword hilt. "Tell me, little man," she said. "What will happen?"

"I...I don't know..."

"Then let's find out."

The Bearer sighed like a dying man breathing his last. He shook so badly, he could barely grasp the quill, but the Book took hold of him in an invisible grip and steadied him as the nib descended on the page. He watched in horror as his hand moved seemingly of its own volition across the map, drawing a clean, impeccable line dividing the land in two.

* * *

Two lovers emerged from the edge of the Aromatic Forest shortly after noon. They walked a short way in silence, smiling into each other's eyes. The young man stopped and reached out to pluck a leaf from his sweetheart's hair. The young woman blushed. "I'd better get back," she said. "Father will be getting suspicious." She took a reluctant step away, her arm outstretched, her fingertips still brushing his. He opened his mouth to reply, but a sudden, deep-seated rumble drowned out his words. The ground swelled between them, thrusting skyward a wall of rock and earth. He flung himself against the barrier, calling her name, but it rewarded him with nothing but dust.

On the Kamankayan Plains, a herd of wild horses stamped and whinnied as the ground shook under their hooves. A piebald stallion reared in defiance at the mountain that suddenly stood in his path. A mare galloped up and down, her call shrill and desperate, while her foal stood shivering and alone on the other side of the wall. On the western coast, fishermen woke from their mid-day siestas to see their moored boats buried under a pile of rubble that extended into the sea. On a farmlet south of the Yacto River, an old woman wailed, her home with her baby grandson asleep inside smashed to pieces from the foundations up as the new formation burst up beneath it.

In the desert, hardened soldiers flung themselves to the ground and whimpered like children as the earth roared and erupted before them, sending an impervious wedge between the two armies. The Bearer sat, balanced precariously in his chair but unharmed, on top of the mountain. The armies looked like fireworks displays to him as they swirled in confusion, their leaders entombed within the huge mound of rubble.

The Bearer hugged the Book ever tighter to his chest and wept.

Ghosts Can Bleed

What do they call those TV shows you love to watch but hate to admit to liking? Guilty pleasures, I believe. My guilty TV pleasure is singing shows, or more specifically, any singing show that involves complete unknowns getting their 15 minutes of fame.

Before the Idol franchise, there was Stars In Their Eyes, a British show whereby wannabes impersonate famous singers. One contestant in particular stuck with me. I don't remember his name, nor who he impersonated, but I will always remember what he did for a living.

His job, for eight hours a day, five days a week, was to check pantyhose for holes. The look on his face as he described his job to his host—well, if Thoreau had been around, he would have said, "Look! Right there! That's exactly the kind of quiet desperation I was talking about!"

That young man had his chance to let his song out. Not so for poor Maurice...

Ghosts can bleed. Maurice knows, because he is one.

His wife, Doreen, can't accept it. "Look," she says, "you cut yourself shaving. That wouldn't happen if you were dead."

"Ghosts are forced to perform the same actions in death as they did in life, over and over again," he tells her for the umpteenth time. "I cut myself shaving at least once a week when I was alive. Why should anything change now?"

Of course, some things have changed. Ghosts can't eat, so he just pushes his toast around his plate with spectral fingers. He gets more and more insubstantial every day, so soon he won't be able to do even that. And he can't make love to Doreen any more. He tried it once, not long after he died. He climbed on top of her and sunk halfway into her body, sucked under by her body fat. Struggling to get out, he got caught up on her ribs. He could feel her heart beating where his used to be, a great, alien, pulsing knot of muscle, and he had to fight to hold down the gorge that no longer existed.

The only other person who can see him is his best friend Charlie. Charlie is a technician at the factory where Maurice used to work. Maurice's job, when he was alive, was to check pantyhose for flaws. Unfurl one leg of the hose onto a flat illuminated glass frame, spin it around to examine it from all sides, repeat with the other leg, and then send the hose down the line for packaging if it was sound, or into the large red bin at his feet if it was not. At the height of his career he could accurately assess up to 1600 pairs of pantyhose a day. Now, improved technology means that the incidences of pantyhose flaws has been reduced to approximately seven a year, a margin of error that management considers low enough to be able to do away with the positions of hose checker altogether.

He still goes to work, though, compelled to do so by the arcane rules that govern the disembodied. Monday through Friday Charlie boards the number 13 bus, with Maurice right behind him. Charlie hands his concession card to the driver and asks her to clip it twice. She hesitates, willing Charlie to come to his senses, then clips it with slow, deliberate care. She shakes her head at Charlie's retreating back as he makes his way down the aisle to the back of the bus.

Maurice sits in his usual seat in the right hand corner in the back row. He has a theory that he only appears to those people in whose lives he made a significant imprint, so he is invisible to the other passengers. Nevertheless, they feel his presence; even on the busiest days, those desperate souls who find themselves at the back glance at Maurice's apparently empty seat, their gaze sliding over him, and invariably opt to stand.

At the factory, Charlie pulls up a chair for Maurice in an unobtrusive spot with a good view of the assembly line. He watches a batch of glossy black 12 Denier Extra Talls zip past on a conveyer belt, row upon row of artificial skins destined to be packaged, shipped, purchased and inhabited.

"You've got to face facts, Maurice," says Charlie. "It's time for you to move on."

Maurice nods. He would move on in a heartbeat if he could. Some days he fancies he can still hear his heartbeat, like the phantom itching in an amputated limb. On those days he feels like he could almost will himself back to life and out of this paranormal rut.

The strain of living in a haunted house becomes too much for Doreen. "I've invited someone to see you," she says.

"Who is it?" he says. "A psychic? A priest? A white witch?"

"A psychiatrist," says Doreen.

"What for? I'm not crazy – I'm dead."

"I've talked to Charlie. He's very concerned about you."

Maurice drifts about the room, scattering magazines and ornaments in his wake. "Maybe you should talk to the psychiatrist. You're the one who can't handle reality."

Doreen starts to cry. Crying does not become her. Her face and chest break out in large crimson blotches, and a small bubble of snot protrudes from her left nostril. "Maurice, you are not dead," she says. "You are very, very unwell."

"You stupid cow!" shouts Maurice. "For the last time – I AM DEAD!" He rushes forward and thrusts his arms through Doreen's head, wiggling his fingers as they emerge out the other side. "See?" he says triumphantly.

Doreen gapes at him for a moment, and then cries louder, her wails high-pitched and liquid. Something shifts inside Maurice, like a misaligned cog slipping into place. Is this the unfinished business he needed to attend to before he could depart the earthly realm – turning his wife into a believer? It's funny; he thought he would be the one to fade away into nothingness. Instead it is Doreen who is becoming less and less distinct, losing substance until she is little more than an outline in the air.

He looks about for a tunnel of light or a welcoming angel or some such sign of his passing. Nothing happens. He is alone in his slightly dishevelled lounge. His body settles around him, bone and muscle and innards and skin, weighing him down until he slumps to the floor. Fading sympathy cards crowd his mantelpiece, and a gust of wind from an open window sends one fluttering down to fall open in his lap. "Dear Maurice," it reads, "we are thinking of you in your time of loss." There is a pain deep in his stomach. It could be anything – hunger, perhaps, or cancer, or grief. Whatever its cause, it is a pain too great for ghosts.

Portrait of The Artist As A Young Mutant

I always said
I'll pay someone to do it
then down the parabola
mutants come
sub-human
sub-marine
I employ a whatsit
with good intentions
to clean my house
walk my dog
watch my kids
It makes do
with cheap sleep
from the Warehouse
writes poetry in its spare time
It writes you
into being
a masterpiece
I keep you for myself
I know it thinks,
and loves, and despairs
but has anyone told God?
For all its skill
it cannot rename itself
the poet drowns in its own prose

Rush Hour

Virgil heard something tapping on the top of his computer monitor. He looked up. His teenaged daughter Ginny looked back at him. Virgil checked his watch.

"Shit! Is it that time already?" he said.

"Language, Dad," Ginny chided.

Virgil's workmate Roger peered over the cubicle wall like a bespectacled meerkat.

"What's up, Virgil?" He feigned surprise. "Oh, hello, Ginny. Didn't see you there. You look lovely in white, as always."

"C'mon, Dad," said Ginny. "You know how bad the drive home can get if we miss the window."

"You should take the bus," Roger said smugly.

They found Virgil's car in the parking building in a row of anonymous Japanese imports, drove down to street level and eased into the traffic. They were moving at a steady pace when the swarm hit. The air was thick with wasps the size of a man's thumb. They splattered against the windscreen. Virgil slowed to a crawl and turned on the wipers, smearing insect gore across the glass. They could just make out the screams of the driver of a convertible one lane over who hadn't been able to get the top up in time.

"Poor sod," muttered Virgil. Ginny tugged at the cross pendant around her neck and said nothing.

Then, as suddenly as the swarm had appeared, it dispersed, blown away by a wind that came up out of nowhere.

"Look," said Ginny. She pointed. "A tornado!" Virgil squinted as he tried to make out where it was centred. The smoky cone spiraled into the air, sucking up debris.

"Oh, God," he said. "It looks like it's over the dump!"

Ginny frowned. "Dad!" she said. "Don't blaspheme!"

The twister passed metres away, pelting cars with jettisoned filth and flipping less fortunate vehicles in its wake. Virgil ducked reflexively as his car shuddered, airborne rubbish bags striking the roof and bonnet. Slow-flowing slime oozed down the windows. A used diaper entangled itself on the wipers. It split, and the wipers laboured across the windscreen as they smeared its contents back and forth. Ginny retched.

"Wasps, tornadoes and shit, and we haven't even made it onto the motorway yet," Virgil muttered. Just as he spoke, the traffic ahead sped up. He loosened his grip a little on the steering wheel as he headed for the on-ramp.

"Watch out for the dog," Ginny said.

"Oh, no – not the dog," Virgil groaned.

The size of a small horse, it stood in the middle of the on-ramp, barking and snapping at car tyres as they swerved to avoid it. It had an impressive strike rate, judging by the number of cars with punctures lining the verges on either side of the road. Not surprising, thought Virgil, considering the mongrel has three heads. A motorcyclist tried to do a U-turn. Virgil snuck past the dog as all three heads were occupied with chewing off the rider's legs at the knees. He looked ahead, and swallowed a curse.

They were approaching the bridge, and things were heating up there – literally. The liquid flowing sluggishly under the bridge was a deep, dirty red. Large bubbles broke the surface. Every now and again a flaming geyser erupted from the river, spilling over the sides of the bridge to engulf passing vehicles. Virgil stopped the car.

"Tell me when," he said to Ginny. "I can never figure out the pattern." Ginny nodded. "3...2...1...go!"

Virgil planted his foot on the accelerator. He cleared the bridge with inches to spare. Heat radiated through the glass from the blast of fire rising up behind them.

The road ran ahead for about five kilometres across a stretch of sandy desert. Ginny gave a low whistle. "They've taken out a bus!" she said. A forty-seater bus lay on its side, several of its tyres pierced with arrows. A herd of centaurs pranced around it, waving their bows in the air. A naked, muscle-bound giant with horns growing from his temples flexed hairy biceps as he forced open the doors and hauled out passengers.

"Isn't that Roger?" asked Ginny. A thin man in a knitted vest sailed through the air and landed awkwardly. He sizzled on contact with the sand. Before he could stand, several vulture-like creatures swooped down on him. Their human faces twisted in fury as they pinned him under their talons and ripped his flesh with jagged teeth. One lifted her head from her meal and hissed at Virgil. Blood dripped down her chin and splattered on her sagging blue-veined breasts.

"You should take the bus," Virgil mimicked savagely. Ginny shot him an offended look and slapped his hand.

Once past the fallen bus, the traffic flow improved. "Looks like rain," Ginny said. Dense black clouds gathered overhead. The air grew oppressively hot. Sweat beaded on Virgil's forehead as he struggled for breath.

"This can't be a good sign," he said.

Fire began to fall from the sky, daintily at first, like the harmless spluttering of a child's sparkler. It intensified until it fell in thick blobs of flame. Ginny closed her eyes and gripped the armrest. Her lips moved in a silent prayer. Virgil fixed his gaze on the road ahead. They emerged out the other side of the downpour with the car's paintwork smoking and scarred, but both occupants unharmed. They slowed to a halt behind a long queue of cars.

"What's the hold-up this time?" Virgil said.

Ginny wound down her window and leant out as far as she could reach. She gasped, pulled back into the car and quickly wound the window back up.

"Road works," she said grimly.

Virgil swallowed hard. His hands trembled slightly. "God help us," he croaked.

"Amen," nodded Ginny.

They crept forward with agonizing slowness. To break the monotony, Virgil turned on the radio. The Rolling Stones' "Sympathy for the Devil" was playing. Ginny snapped the radio off. They continued for the next twenty minutes in silence.

A few cars ahead, Virgil spotted the start of a line of orange cones. Seconds later, they were in chaos. The lane marked out with cones split off in three directions, the new lanes snaking haphazardly across the motorway and intersecting with each other in places. Hulking man-like creatures in fluorescent yellow vests stood at irregular intervals. Green drool dripped from their grinning maws as they randomly spun Stop/Go signs, sending confused motorists into slow-motion collisions. A couple of drivers got out of their cars to swap insurance details. Virgil leant on his horn.

"Look out behind you!" he shouted. He pointed at a crew of bony little purple-skinned men wheeling a steaming cauldron into place be-hind the unsuspecting drivers. One turned around in time to see the men tip the cauldron over. Hot tar spilt over the road, pooling around the driver's ankles. They screamed and frantically tried to extract them-selves, but more mutant road workers were on hand to prod them with pitchforks until they overbalanced, sprawling face-first into the tar. The little purple men applauded, waving their forked tails with glee. A bull-dozer rumbled forward to push the abandoned cars out of the way, col-lecting several occupied vehicles in the process.

"We'll never make it," Virgil said.

"Have a little faith," said Ginny. "They must be due for a smoko break any minute."

As if on cue, all the workers dropped their tools. Some took out ther-mos flasks and poured themselves steaming cups of excrement. Others produced cigarette packets. One creature leant over and lit his cigarette on the burning flesh of his last victim. Virgil avoided their eyes as he picked a tortuous path through the site.

They emerged into an eerie scene of calm. The last of the daylight abruptly fled, and with it went the sweltering heat from the road works. The car's headlights struggled to penetrate the darkness. Virgil shivered in the sudden cold. The car slipped and slid on ice coating the road. They didn't see the figure in the middle of the road until they were al-most on top of him.

He stood nearly nine feet tall. At first Virgil thought he was wear-ing a full-length black coat, but then the man flexed his shoulders and opened up two magnificent ebony wings. All Virgil could see of his face was his glowing red eyes. Virgil stared, mesmerized. His hands slid nervelessly from the wheel.

Ginny sighed. She leant over her father, pressed his right leg gently onto the accelerator, and awkwardly took control of the steering with her left hand. As they rolled past, the winged man lost eye contact with Virgil. He shook himself awake and took over from Ginny. She looked out the back window and gave the retreating figure the finger.

In an instant they were in suburbia. Virgil turned into their street, then into their driveway. The streetlights cast a benign yellow glow around Ginny's head as she got out of the car. Virgil's wife greeted them at the door. He kissed her cheek.

"Sorry we're late, love," he said. "The traffic was hell."

Metal Mouth

Ah, who can ever forget their first paid acceptance...

"Get your arses back here, ya mongrels!"

Carl's dogs looked back at him, tongues lolling, then plunged on through the bush. Carl hefted the pig's carcass over his back and started up the slope after them. His jaw throbbed with the effort. The last time he'd been hunting, he'd stumbled across a couple of blokes tending their cannabis plot. He'd got a good look at one of them, a dreadlocked dickhead with a face full of piercings, before his mate smacked the side of Carl's face in with a baseball bat. Six months later he still had a mouth full of wire holding his jaw together.

As he neared the top of the ridge, he turned on the radio slung around his neck. Should be able to pick up something here, he thought. He had fifty bucks riding on the game this weekend, and he wanted to find out the score. He surfed the static until he picked up a patchy reception.

"...succeeded in repelling the alien invasion...some could still be at large.... report any sightings to the following number..."

Must've picked up some bullshit radio play, he thought. He thumbed the dial through the frequencies, finding only more static, then switched it off.

He was nearly at the edge of the track where his ute was parked when his dogs came back, circling around his heels. He frowned. Normally they would be sitting on the back waiting for him. If some bastard had stolen it, he'd...

Carl stopped. The pig slid off his back. "Fuck me sideways!"

His ute was still there – what was left of it. The tyres sat on the ground, peeled from the missing rims like orange rinds. Between them lay the disembowelled seat. The steering wheel, gear stick and most of the dashboard were all largely intact. Shattered glass and shreds of bright plastic insulation decorated the site. Not a trace of metal remained. The dogs nosed through the debris, whining. Carl's hands shook with fury as he loaded his rifle.

Movement flickered on the edge of his vision. Carl turned to see two creatures emerging from the scrub. The largest stood about eight feet tall. Its neck and shoulders were heavily muscled to support a massive head and elongated jaws. Its skin was dappled grey like a leprous elephant hide, but smooth and glossy. The dogs went into a barking frenzy from the relative safety of Carl's heels.

Carl took aim and fired. The creatures didn't flinch. The bullet lodged in the centre of the largest creature's forehead like a third eye. It reached up and calmly extracted the bullet. Its flesh smoothed over to leave no trace of the impact. The creature examined the bullet, sniffed at it, and popped it in its mouth. The two creatures seemed to confer silently. They dropped to all fours, and in a blur of movement covered the several metres between themselves and Carl before he could blink.

The larger of the pair knocked him down and pinned him to the ground with one knee. It plucked his rifle from his grip and tossed it to its mate, who snapped it in two. They ate half each, the crunching sounding like a slow motion car crash. Carl caught a glimpse of triple rows of finger-length serrated metallic grey fangs.

The dogs were by now hysterical. Bess, his huntaway-boxer cross bitch, darted in to attack Carl's captor. It picked her up by the scruff of the neck and sniffed her all over. Bess's teeth slid off the creature's skin as if she were trying to bite a windowpane.

Carl struggled impotently. "Let her go, you fucking freak!" he yelled.

Two glinting talons extruded from the creature's free hand. It severed Bess's collar and let her drop. She hit the ground awkwardly, then scrabbled to her feet and headed for the hills, her mate close behind. The creature pulled the buckle of the collar free from the leather and swallowed it whole.

The two creatures returned their attention to Carl. The leader subjected him to the same sniff test it had given Bess. Again claws extended from its fingers. It drew two delicate lines down his chest, neatly removing the zipper from his jacket. It slurped up the zipper, chewed thoughtfully, then turned its head to the side and spat out remnants of cloth. Meanwhile, the smaller creature plucked all the eyelets from his boots. If they keep going, thought Carl, they're going to meet in the middle and start scrapping over my...

Frantically Carl fumbled with his belt buckle and slid his jeans down his thighs. The creatures shredded his belt and jeans, extracting buckle, zip and studs. They rumbled in appreciation at the discovery of his hunting knife in the back pocket. The larger creature lifted its knee from Carl's chest. Carl scrambled to his feet and started to run, when he heard the distant whine of trail bikes. Kids, he thought. Bloody kids. "Get out of here, you idiots! Fuck off!" he yelled.

The creature spun back on him. It gripped the front of his shirt, pulled Carl close to its muzzle and inhaled deeply. It prized Carl's jaw open, its slanted eyes widening at the sight of the metal scaffolding in his mouth. It hooked a talon into the wire and tugged. Carl half-screamed, half-gargled in pain.

The whine became a roar as two motorcycles skidded into view. The creature dropped Carl and bounded after them, its companion on its heels. The bikes' riders fell heavily as the creatures took them down. One lay immobile, apparently unconscious. The second man screamed, clutching his leg. Carl thought he looked familiar. The tongue stud, the pierced eyebrow, the ring in the nose, the shoulder-length brown dreadlocks...

Carl gathered what remained of his clothes, and grinned. He waved at the creatures. "Make sure you save room for dessert, fuckers!" he called, and slipped into the bush after his dogs.

Barking

This story is one of my earliest, written as part of my course work for my Diploma of Creative Writing. The brief was to write "a story within a story". I'm fond of the piece, for two reasons -

a) It's one of the first times I drew on personal experience and twisted it beyond recognition to produce a piece of fiction (somebody did once pull that trick on me in the pub. But he wasn't a pharmaceutical sales rep, and I didn't sleep with him).

b) It's also one of the few times I have practiced what Holly Lisle calls "Mugging the Muse". I was pregnant and/or breastfeeding during the entire three years it took to complete my diploma. I also worked nights and weekends. I was in a constant state of sleep deprivation. But I had a deadline to meet. I sat down one night, gritted my teeth and wrote until 1 a.m. until I had a complete first draft.

You want to know when my problems started? You tell me, you're the shrink.

Sorry. Didn't mean to bite your head off. It's just I've been under a lot of pressure lately. But don't even think about prescribing me drugs. I'm a sales rep for a pharmaceutical company, so I know more than you do about the side effects that shit can cause.

You reckon hypnotherapy might help? Well, it's funny you should say that. *Really* funny, because it was a story about a dog and a hypnotist that got me in the trouble I'm in. What kind of trouble? You don't want to know. OK, you're a psychiatrist, so I suppose you *do* want to know. And you know what they say; time is money, so I'd better get on with it.

It started a few months ago when I was on my Far North sales trip. After checking in to my hotel, I headed down to the local watering hole. It was dead quiet, with maybe five or six other people in the bar and I was thinking about having an early night, when in walked these two girls. They were both wearing faded jeans, boots and buttoned up shirts, like they'd just won first prize in a synchronised dressing contest. One of them was average, instantly forgettable, but the other one – well, she looked like she was wearing Jeans In A Can, you know, practically spray painted on, and she had long, strawberry blonde hair that almost met up with her cleavage. It was enough to make me give my wedding ring a nervous twist.

I ordered another beer and tried not to look at the girls, but they must have been as bored as I was, because the plain one came over and asked if I wanted to join them in a game of pool. So I said sure, why not? I bought a round of drinks and played it cool for a while, shooting pool and making small talk. After a while the plain girl wandered off to talk to some of her mates, and I was left alone with the pretty one. We were talking, she was laughing, and I was feeling like hot shit on toast after four or five beers. Before I knew it I was launching into this yarn I used to spin back in my single days.

I asked her, do you believe in reincarnation?

She gave me a half-smile and leant away from me slightly, as if my madness might be catching. So I said, I never used to, until I went to this hypnotherapist a few years ago to help me give up smoking. One of my workmates had recommended him, reckoned he was a real magician. Anyway, it turned out that, not only could he help people to stop biting their nails or to lose weight, stuff like that, but he was a whiz at regressive therapy – you know, where they take you back to relive traumatic events in your past. AND – he was psychic.

She was looking at me by this stage with her pale blue eyes wide as a baby's, and she'd leant back in, totally hooked. I told her, yeah, I bet you're thinking, what a load of crap, right? Well, within seconds he had me in a trance, and when I came around, he was looking at me as if I'd sprouted an extra head. He said that while I was under, I had started regressing, going back to my childhood, and that I just kept going, back and back, as far back as the womb and then further, back into my past lives.

The girl whispered noooo! And I said, it's true, it's all true! I was getting into it so much by now, I almost believed it myself.

Do you want to know what he told me? I said. He said that in one of my past lives, I had been a dog.

The girl stared at me with her mouth open for a moment, then she laughed and punched me on the arm, and said, you're a bit of a dog now.

I know, it sounds totally unreal, I said, but you gotta hear the rest of it. He said that, with a combination of hypnotherapy and psychic connection, he found out that I had been a guard dog for a Roman senator. Apparently I'd been a bull mastiff, you know, one of those huge bloody things with no neck and a head the size of a lion's, kind of a canine Bull Allen. Apparently I had come to a violent end in that life when one of my master's enemies bludgeoned me over the head with an iron-spiked club. And I said to the girl, do you want to know what the weirdest thing about that is? Right where he said I got hit over the head in my past life, I've got a dent in my skull in this one. Do you want to feel it?

Well, I could tell she *didn't* want to feel it, but I took her hand and guided it up to my head. That was when I first felt a bit guilty, because her hands were so tiny, I felt like I was teasing a child. She brushed those little fingers over my skull as if it was a hot plate, then she realised that there really was a dip there. I got it in a biking accident when I was a teenager, showing off on my BMX without a helmet, but I wasn't going to tell her that. She stood on tiptoe to get a better look at my skull, which gave me a good look down her shirt, and I knew I had her.

When she couldn't get any closer without smothering me, I barked at her, as loudly and ferociously as I could. Well, you should have seen her jump! She nearly wet herself. Then just when I thought I'd gone too far and she was going to cry, she tipped over into laughter.

At this point, I thought, I am in serious trouble. I always say there are only two things that will get a girl into bed - laughter and fear, and I'd triggered both of them.

Oh, OK, and money, make that three things. But I've never paid for it in my life, and I was guessing she was the kind of girl who gave it away for free.

Her favours weren't entirely no-strings-attached, as it turned out. Once she'd finished laughing, she nestled up close to me and whispered in my ear, did I have any drug samples on me that she might be interested in? I took her down to my car and put together a little pharmaceutical cocktail that I thought she might enjoy. No, don't look at me like that. It wasn't as if I'd spiked her drink or anything. She *asked* for it.

I don't remember much about what happened next. We must have got pretty wasted, because next thing you know we're back at my hotel room and I'm peeling those skin-tight jeans off her and throwing her on to the bed.

So, like I said, we were both hammered to bits, and I was fucking her but not doing a very good job of it, and she was trying not to show that she wasn't enjoying it. And I realised that she wasn't really attracted to me, not physically, she was only there because, oh, I don't know, because I made her laugh, or because she'd been brought up to never say "no", or because she had nothing better to do. I was already feeling sick from the booze, and guilty for cheating on my wife, and then I started to get angry.

Now, I'm not normally an angry man. Honestly, I'm not. But there was something about this girl's passiveness that got to me. I thought I'd managed to keep my feelings to myself, but I guess I wasn't too successful. The next morning she staggered out of bed, groaning with what she said was the worst hangover she'd ever had. I noticed bruises coming up on her thighs and fresh bite marks on her breasts, and when she turned away from me, I saw thick red welts striping her back.

She was in such a hurry to get away from me, she put her knickers on inside out and buttoned up her shirt crooked. At this point, I didn't realise that I had been the one to hurt her. I thought that maybe she had some violent boyfriend she had to hurry home to. I asked her, could I help her, give her a lift home or maybe money for a taxi? She shot me this look of contempt, like my wife does when I forget to put out the rubbish, and said sarcastically, I'd given her more than enough, thanks very much. As she walked out, she called me a fucking animal. I almost looked over my shoulder to see who she was talking to, until it got through my thick skull that I was the animal.

Well, what could I do? I got up and showered and threw down a couple of cups of instant coffee and some Panadol, then I went about my day as if nothing had happened, all the while going over the night before and trying to figure out what went wrong. When I got home, I started telling my wife the edited highlights of my trip, when the cat came barrelling through the cat flap, took one look at me, skidded to a halt and started hissing. You know, back arched, hackles raised, tail bristled, the whole bit. My guts started churning, thinking that maybe my wife had trained the cat to sniff out other women on me. It crossed my mind that it was time for the cat to meet with an "accident", but then I told myself, don't be stupid, that's just your guilt talking. Sure, I'd never liked that cat, but I don't like my mother-in-law either, and she's still alive, more's the pity.

I had a typically uneventful weekend, a bit of gardening, a bit of shopping, rented a couple of videos on Saturday night, that sort of thing. I had a couple of beers with the videos, and I remember thinking, Jeez, I must be getting out of practice, because I felt like I'd washed down half a dozen sedatives with them. I went to bed early and woke up with aching muscles in my neck and shoulders. I thought I was probably coming down with the 'flu, so I lounged around the house until I started to come right.

Later that night the wife realised that she hadn't seen the cat for a couple of days. She remembered how it had acted weird when I came home on Friday and thought that maybe it was sick, so she sent me out with a torch to look for it. Well, I found it, all right. It was in a corner behind the garage, dead. Its neck was broken, as if someone or something had picked it up and literally shaken the life out of it. I knew my wife would freak if she saw it, so I wrapped it in a plastic bag and stuffed it in the boot of my car to dispose of later. I told my wife I couldn't find it.

The next couple of days were much like the weekend, nothing out of the ordinary, then came Wednesday. My wife goes to Thai cooking classes at the local high school on Wednesdays, so I'm left to my own devices. Usually I order myself a pizza, have a few drinks, put my feet on the coffee table and channel surf. But on this particular night I had a craving for steak. So I stopped at the supermarket on the way home, bought myself a ten dollar T-bone, took it home and got out the biggest frying pan we own.

I started to take the steak out of its Styrofoam tray – then everything went black. It only seemed like a second or two, but when I came around, the pan was smoking on the stove, just about to combust, and I was chewing into this steak *raw*. Blood was dripping down my arms and soaking into my shirt. I'd almost finished the meat and had started gnawing on the bone before I realised what I was doing. I thought I was going to puke, except I didn't want to waste all that good steak. So there I was, soaking my shirt, washing it and throwing it in the dryer, mopping up the floor, sneaking around again so my wife didn't know what going on. Christ, even I didn't know what was going on.

Nothing else weird happened for a couple of weeks. Then Lockhead came back to work.

James Lockhead. He's a sales manager. I can't stand the smarmy bastard. He'd been on leave, and I'd been doing his job while he was away. He'd barely walked through the door when he started in on me about the sales figures being down or some such crap. He poked me in the chest with his finger, I gave him a shove to make him back up, he shoved me back, and before I knew it, we were having an all-out brawl.

Now, like I said, I'm usually an even-tempered man. I wouldn't have bit him if he hadn't punched me in the eye first. I think I was aiming for his throat, but luckily he turned his head at the right time, and I sunk my teeth into his left ear and did a Mike Tyson on him. Took a chunk clean out.

It was complete chaos. James was screaming and clutching the side of his head, there was blood pissing out everywhere, I was snarling like an animal, a couple of the other reps were holding me back, and I think the receptionist had fainted. James started bellowing at the nearest office junior to find his missing piece of ear and pack it in ice so it could be reattached. The poor little thing was scrabbling around under the desks and crying, terrified that she wasn't going to find it and terrified that she was. Her skirt hitched up as she crawled about and I got a couple of eyefuls of her lace-pantied arse. I didn't know what I wanted to do more, kill James or jump on that girl. She never did find that piece of ear, because I'd swallowed it.

Once Lockhead had gone to hospital, I got hauled to the General Manager's office and he sent me home for the rest of the week. He said he'd speak to me in a couple of days when we had all calmed down. Of course, the shit hit the fan when I got home. News of what had happened had gone through the office like wildfire and spread to neighbouring buildings as well, and my wife's best friend worked for the accounting firm next door. She rang my wife as soon as she heard, so by the time I walked in the front door, my wife had my bags packed. I tried to tell her it was all exaggerated, but she didn't believe me. Not surprising, considering I had a black eye and another bloke's blood all over me.

My wife kicks me out at least four times a year, so I did what I always do. I went to stay at my mate Colin's place. I like staying at Colin's. His couch is comfortable, he drinks the same brand of beer as me, and he's got a great porn collection. Sometimes I pick a fight with the missus on purpose so I can go stay at Colin's. I didn't go into details, just told him the wife and I had had a falling out. He must have thought I was nuts, though, when he said, "So, you're in the dog box, are you?" and I nearly choked on my Steinlager.

I stayed with Colin for two weeks. That was how long it took to get a new job with another pharmaceutical company and get back in the wife's good books. That wasn't hard once she heard that my new job came with a hefty pay rise. It's a small world, this industry – my new boss had heard about the ear-biting incident, and he hates James Lockhead too. So I thought, maybe this personality change I'm experiencing isn't such a bad thing. Might make me a more aggressive salesman or something.

Or something, it turned out. Everything was going along nicely, my new job was great, my wife was being civil to me, and I thought my life was back on track. And then I had this nightmare.

Jesus, it was frightening, it was so vivid. I dreamt I was running through a forest. The perspective was all screwed up, it was like I was only three feet tall, but running faster than I've ever been able to move before. I could see my breath clouding out in front of me. The smell of pine needles was so strong, it was almost burning my nostrils. And you know the way you just *know* things in your dreams, without having to see them or have it spelt out to you? Well, I knew I was chasing something. And I was getting closer.

In the dream, I ran into a clearing, and I saw a little grey rabbit run into the forest on the other side. I pushed myself to go faster, and then I was on it. I felt this huge adrenaline rush as I tore into the rabbit's back and heard it squeal in agony. I was ripping it to bits, spraying blood and fur in all directions, and somewhere in the distance I could hear someone calling my name, frantically trying to call me off the rabbit, only hearing that voice made me even more vicious. It was like I knew that, once the person calling caught up with me, that would be it. I'd get chained up, and I'd never get a chance to hunt again.

When I woke up, I was panting and drenched in sweat, and I had this strange metallic taste in my mouth. I turned on the bedside light, and then I looked down and saw that I was covered in blood. It was everywhere, soaking the sheets, splattering the walls, and starting to congeal in my chest hair. I nearly had a heart attack when I saw it. I thought someone must've stabbed me in my sleep. I couldn't feel any pain, but all that blood had to have come from somewhere, right? I gave myself a frantic pat-down, but I couldn't find any injuries, so I started to breathe easier then.

I looked at my wife to see if I had woken her up. She was lying next to me naked, completely still, and staring up at the ceiling with unblinking eyes. Her arms were flung up, covering the lower part of her face. She was so messed up, it looked like someone had taken to her with a claw hammer. I could hear a steady drip, drip, drip of blood that was seeping from a ragged, fist-sized hole in her throat.

I got out of there quick smart. I didn't stop to dress, to wash, nothing, just scooped up my car keys and took off. I drove around aimlessly at first, shaking and crying and generally acting like the world's biggest two-year-old, until it came to me what I needed to do.

I cruised along the back streets until I reached the beach, then I got out of the car and ran into the water to clean myself up. I nearly froze my balls off, it was so cold. I ran into this drunk guy staggering home from a party as I was getting out of the water, and he was so surprised to see a naked bloke walking up the beach at 2 a.m. on a winter's morning, he didn't even put his hands up to defend himself when I mugged him for his clothes and wallet.

That was a couple of nights ago. And now here I am, feeling lucky you could fit me in at such short notice, otherwise you would have read about what happened to my wife in the papers by now and you'd be on the phone to the cops.

So what do you reckon, doctor – am I going mad, or what? Don't worry, I'm not going to hurt you. Or maybe I am. I don't know any more.

No, don't try to tell me you're not afraid of me. I can smell fear, you know.

Offspring

We gave them breath
To call their own
But they flew too high
Too far, too soon
Circling our sun
Howling at our moon
They melted in the heat
Of their own brilliance
So we played
On their bones
Until the very walls
Joined us in dance
Then dropped
To sleep
To dream
In their ashes.

Flesh Pot

Dan sat up and groaned. His head hurt. What happened last night? He remembered drinking at the spaceport bar. He'd been playing snooker with two soldiers fresh from an off-world tour of duty, and he remembered winning a lot, in spite of (or perhaps because of) his increasing drunkenness. He remembered the soldiers talking in graphic detail about their experiences in a nearby brothel staffed by extra-terrestrials. When he had confessed to being an alien sex "virgin", they had laughed, promised to introduce him to such illicit pleasures. He vaguely recalled the soldiers lugging him like a meat-stuffed sack out of the bar at the end of the night, and then... nothing. He put his hand up to his throbbing temples, and felt two small metallic studs burrowed into each side of his skull. He probed the implants with his fingertips, and yelped as he touched freshly pierced skin.

A feminine voice sounded inside his head.

I put them there so we can... talk. Now, keep still. I have to peel you.

Dan looked up. A blue-furred creature stood over him. He squealed and skittered backwards. The creature's face did not change expression, but he heard her giggle.

Not your skin, silly. A sound like static filled his head as she struggled to find the right words. *Your... robes.*

She must have read his mind to know his immediate fear, just as he was hearing her voice in his mind. Neat trick, he thought. Pity it involved drilling into his brain to do it.

Dan studied her. She was about the same height as him. Her eyes were huge, literally saucer-sized, and dominated her triangular face. Her nostrils were almost hidden by the short pale blue fur that covered her body. He couldn't see a mouth. She stood on two oddly jointed legs that ended in small hooves. She had two vestigial arms with seven stubby digits on each. Her only clothing was a large iridescent plate wrapped around her slender chest. Her fingers played over it continuously, sending eddies of colour across its surface.

121

He switched his attention to his surroundings. They were in a cavernous room, completely devoid of furniture. Off-white walls curved away almost out of sight above him. There weren't any doors or windows that he could see. It was as if he was inside a gigantic egg.

The wall suddenly oozed out at him. It stretched and hardened into several arms. Four arms wrapped around his wrists and ankles to immobilize him, and three more formed long elastic fingers that deftly stripped him of his clothes. He struggled uselessly against the restraints.

Don't worry, came the voice. *This won't hurt.*

Dan's skin crept at the emphasis she placed on "this". Bondage and Discipline wasn't his thing, at least not if he was on the receiving end. He wondered how much this was going to cost. Hopefully his soldier mates had put some money on his tab. He tried to relax. Sex was sex, even if it was with some furry blue freak. He looked at the alien through half-lidded eyes and tried to find something attractive about her. Did she even have sex organs under that fur, he wondered.

The alien cocked her head to one side.

What is...sex?

This had better be cheap, Dan thought, if she doesn't even know what sex is.

"It's how humans reproduce," he explained. "And have fun. What about your people? How do they make babies?"

I'm not sure. I'd have to ask my...

The wall behind her parted, cutting off her thought. A second alien entered the room. It was identical to the first, except that it was twice the size. The two faced each other and held what looked like a heated mind conversation, their fingers blurring over their chest plates. Dan's mind filled with white noise, cutting him out of the loop. The larger alien left, leaving the walls seamless again, and Dan's mind abruptly cleared.

"What was that all about?" he said.

She didn't reply at first. A long fleshy tube, like an elephant's trunk, extruded from where Dan guessed her stomach would be. A few drops of clear liquid dripped from the end of the tube and splashed onto his foot. He screamed in agony as the substance burnt into his flesh. When she finally answered him, he detected through his terror a note of petulance.

Mother says I must not play with my food.

Whipping Boy

Candice had been gone from her home town for too long. It had changed, and it had taken her three months of working at the Grand Hotel to figure out what the difference was. The clientele of the hotel were as rough as she remembered; dairy farms and the fish factory were the main employers in the area, and most of the customers didn't bother to scrape the cow shit or the fish guts off their gumboots before they came inside. And they all drank more heavily than the fish they spent their days disembowelling. Yet the closest she had come to witnessing a bar brawl was when Chloe Baker threw a dart at the back of Julie Bennett's head for flirting with Chloe's boyfriend (she missed). She'd seen more aggro in a week in the upmarket bar she'd last worked in than she'd seen here. It should have been a good thing, but something about the vibe in the town unsettled her.

For the umpteenth time that night, she snuck a glance at the man sitting in the corner. Candice thought she knew everybody in this town, and if she didn't, she knew their cousin or their parents or their spouse, or whoever was responsible for bringing them here. But he didn't seem to be connected to anybody. He looked to be about her age, in his mid-thirties, with dusty shoulder-length dreadlocks, a dancer's bearing, and eyes so pale a shade of blue they were almost colourless. He came in every night at the same time and sat in the same corner until closing, watching the other patrons with a faint smile on his face that made him look sometimes like an idiot, sometimes like a saint. He never bought anything, but had a constant supply of rum and cokes supplied to him by the other customers, who would greet him with a deferential nod or raised eyebrow, leave the drink on his table like an offering on an altar, and retreat to leave him alone. Despite clearly being the most attractive man in the pub, nobody, man or woman, ventured to hit on him. And, no matter what the weather, he always wore gloves. Candice imagined all manner of disfigurements beneath the glossy black leather. Then she imagined those hands caressing her naked body. She couldn't decide whether the thought aroused or repulsed her.

"What's the deal with him?" Candice asked Trevor one night, jerking her head towards the stranger. "Everyone seems to be a little scared of him. Is he a drug lord hiding out or something?"

"Who, Zero?" her boss replied. He looked at the man, then at the ceiling, then at the glass he was polishing. "Nah, it's nothing like that. He's just…a bloke minding his own business." *Much like you should*, was the unspoken rebuke.

"Is that his name? Zero? Weird name for a weird bloke, if you ask me."

Trevor grunted and rubbed harder at an invisible spot on the glass. "You can take off now if you like," he said. "I'll finish up here."

Candice eyed him suspiciously as she scooped up her handbag and jacket. If he wouldn't tell her the truth about Zero, she'd find someone who would. She might even ask him directly. The thought of confronting the mystery man set her stomach swirling, and she rushed out the door before Trevor could see the colour rising in her face.

* * *

"Don't start on me. I just want to have a few quiet drinks with my mates. Anyway, you can't stop me. I'm eighteen now, remember?"

Candice glared at her son, Aaron. Trevor leant across her and handed Aaron a beer before she could open her mouth to protest.

"On the house. Happy birthday, mate."

Oblivious for a moment to the press of customers at the bar, Candice watched her son join his friends. It had been at Aaron's suggestion that they move back here, dragging her out of an increasingly dangerous drug scene. He'd always been the more responsible of the two; he must have been the only kid she knew who stole money from his mother's purse to put aside to pay the power bill. Things had finally come to a head when a violent confrontation with her dealer had ended with Aaron being hospitalised. Maybe it was too little, too late, but the least she could do was return the favour and start looking out for him for a change.

Misreading her scowl, Trevor nudged her and said, "You can't protect him forever." She nodded and moved away to serve the raucous knot of women out on a hen's night at the other end of the bar. She tried to put Aaron out of her mind, to think of him as just another customer, and had almost succeeded when two uniformed policemen came in and began to wend their way through the crowd. They headed for Zero's table first, exchanging a few pleasantries, chose several other men in the crowd to speak to, seemingly at random, then backtracked to stop at Aaron's table. She recognised the older cop as he bent his six foot six frame in half to speak into Aaron's ear. David Bowman. Candice had had a crush on him in high school, but looking now at his gangly body and long, horsy face, she couldn't for the life of her remember why. She left her post behind the bar to follow them, but by the time she had elbowed halfway through the forest of warm bodies, the cops were exiting past her.

"What was that all about?" she demanded.

"Nothing you need to worry about," Aaron said. His face was flushed, and his eyes shone with a fervour that couldn't be put down to the two beers he'd consumed. "Dave just wanted to wish me a happy birthday."

"Since when have you been on first name terms with cops?"

"Since when have you cared?" he shot back.

Aaron's friends sniggered. One of them checked his watch. "Time to go, bro."

"Is Aaron allowed out to play?" another one asked Candice, prompting a fresh round of guffaws from the group. They got up as one and pushed past her.

The other men Dave Bowman had spoken to were also leaving in twos and threes. She was all too familiar with this scenario, and wasn't overly surprised that the local cop was involved. Zero got up and followed after them. She noticed that he didn't have to jostle anyone to get out, the crowd parting around him to let him pass untouched. It looked like her original assessment about Zero was correct. Why Aaron was letting himself get dragged into it, she had no idea.

But more importantly, she was getting left out.

Candice moved into Zero's slipstream and ducked back behind the bar to grab her handbag.

"Sorry, Trevor, gotta go. Women's trouble." She waved her hands in the direction of her abdomen. "And I think I've got a stomach bug. I could...you know...at any minute." She rushed out the door without waiting for his response.

* * *

Candice kept a discreet distance back from the car carrying her son. With the number of other vehicles also travelling over the winding dirt road that led to the coast, this was more than just a few blokes ducking outside for a few quick tokes round the back of the pub. A hydroponics operation, perhaps, or a meth lab, or maybe even a cocaine shipment coming in from the sea. It was way out of her league, and she would have turned back, except...

He would be there.

She shook her head vigorously. Admit it, girl, she said to herself, you're obsessed with him. Experience told her that if she was that interested in a man, it usually meant he was bad news. And when this bad news also involved Aaron, the police and the possibility of a drug score, she was going to be there.

To do what, exactly? a cynical voice in her head asked. Her hands tightened around the steering wheel as she negotiated a particularly sharp corner. She'd just have to make it up as she went along.

She followed the others to stop at the edge of a clearing, parked a short distance away from them and hunched down in her seat, listening to the tick of her car's engine as it cooled. When she was sure all the other cars sat unoccupied, she got out and stepped gingerly through the darkness in the direction of the voices.

Light shone from a derelict shearing shed, and she crept around the back of it to peer through a grimy window. The interior of the shed belied its unkempt outer appearance. Fluorescent light tubes hung above the pool table that dominated the centre. Several old but comfortable looking vinyl armchairs dotted the perimeter, along with a fold-out sofa bed. A makeshift kitchen had been set up in one corner. The cords powering a fridge, microwave, kettle and toaster formed a hazardous tangle on the floor. The opposite corner was curtained off, concealing, Candice guessed, a toilet and shower. She counted fifteen men gathered inside. Aaron was there. So was Dave Bowman, still in his uniform, and Alan Fuller, the owner of the fish factory, who was rarely seen outside of his six-bedroom mansion on the outskirts of town. No music, no booze, no women.

And, Candice realised with a sick feeling, they were all armed.

Each man held some kind of club. Candice counted three baseball bats, an axe handle, a hammer and two metal pokers. Aaron had a tyre iron. One young man held a branch that still leaked sap from where it had been torn from a tree. He hefted it from hand to hand, gripping it at different points along its length as if testing for the most comfortable hold.

The curtain in the corner slid back, and Zero stepped into view. He was naked from the waist up, and Candice drew in a breath at the sight of his lean, tightly muscled torso. His hands were also bare, and they looked as perfectly formed as the rest of him. Bearing his customary smile, he spread his arms wide and slowly turned through a circle. The other men tensed and raised their weapons. Zero stopped face to face with Aaron.

"First blood goes to you, my friend."

Aaron looked at Dave for assurance, and the cop nodded. His face solemn, Aaron took a step back, and swung his tyre iron with full force into Zero's ribs, the men's whooping war cries drowning out the crack of splintering bone. Candice whimpered and turned away, clamping her hands over her ears to block out the stomach-churning sound of fifteen blunt instruments thudding into one unprotected body. There was no way anyone could survive such an attack. She couldn't even call the cops, she thought, fighting back hysteria. They were already here.

She forced herself to look through the window again. Zero lay unmoving on his side on the pool table, his skin tattooed in blood and bruises. The men swung their weapons overhead as they continued to strike him. They looked like children bashing at a piñata, and she choked back bile as she envisioned Zero's innards bursting from him like macabre party favours. He must be dead, she thought, but then he languidly opened his eyes and looked straight at her. There was no pain or fear in his expression, only a kind of resigned sadness, and for a moment she transcended her terror and teetered on the brink of an epiphany. Almost imperceptibly, he shook his head at her, and closed his eyes. The connection broke, panic overwhelmed her, and she curled up sobbing on the ground.

* * *

The sound of running water and someone boisterously singing a Bob Marley song penetrated Candice's fear-fogged brain. Her stiff limbs protested as she stood and dared to look through the window. The room appeared empty, and the pool table where Zero had lain was bare except for a few ominous looking stains. In the clearing visible beyond the open door, her car sat alone. She swore under her breath. If any of the men had noticed her car when they left, she was dead meat. The running water stopped, and so did the singing. Before she could react, a face appeared in the window. Candice started backwards in fright.

It was Zero—alive and whole, and clad only in a towel wrapped around his waist. His skin was smooth, tanned and flawless. They stared at each other for a few moments, then he shrugged and beckoned her inside. She rounded the side of the shed and stood trembling on the threshold, too terrified to enter and too intrigued not to. He met her at the door, more modestly dressed in jeans and a T shirt, and ushered her outside to a lopsided picnic table illuminated by a row of citronella candles.

"Where do we start?" he mused almost to himself.

"Why aren't you dead?" Candice blurted. Zero laughed.

"You sound disappointed! Here–I'll show you a little trick." He got up and went inside, then returned with a small paring knife. He sat down next to her and laid his left arm on the table between them, wrist facing up.

"Watch," he said. He plunged the knife up to the hilt into his wrist and held up his arm to show the blade protruding from the other side. Candice yelped and reached out to stop him, but he jerked away from her and slid backwards along the seat. He dragged the knife slowly downward until it reached the crook of his elbow. Candice whimpered as he pushed his fingers through the gaping wound in his arm and waggled them at her.

"Now, keep watching." He withdrew his hand. The coppery scent of his blood almost overwhelmed her. She dug her fingernails into the edge of the table and bit her lip, compelling herself not to faint. The edges of the wound were visibly knitting together, until, in a matter of minutes, his arm was whole and unmarked. He casually rubbed away the remaining traces of blood on his shirt.

"Neat trick, isn't it?" he said. "At least, Dave Bowman thought so. He pulled me out of a car wreck a year or so back and saw me regenerate." He looked away from her, as if lost in the memory of the accident, and Candice saw the same look of sorrow in his face he had shown when he was being beaten. Then he seemed to gather himself up, and when he turned back to her he was the picture of genial innocence.

"So what's with your little 'fight club'?" Candice said. "Just because you can survive being beaten to a bloody pulp doesn't mean that you should."

"Ah, but that's just the point," said Zero. "I'm actually doing these men a valuable service by allowing them to take their frustrations out on me. You see, Dave has this theory—and from what I know of human nature, I agree with him—that human beings are inherently violent by nature. Most people are strong enough to control it, but some aren't. They have to take it out on someone, and if they weren't taking it out on me, then their wives, or their children, or their dog, or some poor bastard down the pub that accidentally splashed their pint on their shoes, would be getting the bash."

Candice thought of the savagery in her son's face when he had attacked Zero, and her eyes pricked with tears. Angrily, she rubbed them away.

"Do you think that makes you some kind of hero? Some kind of Jesus figure, suffering for their sins?" she snapped.

Zero laughed. "Me? A Jesus figure? Far from it. I have my own sins to suffer for. Anyway, I don't suffer at all—at least not in the way that you think."

"Then why do you do it?"

"I have a place here. I provide a service, and in return, people let me live my life in peace. Nobody treats me as a freak—not much, anyway."

"But... but there's got to be something better than living in a rundown old shed in the back of beyond. With what you can do, I bet you could make tons of money."

Zero snorted. "In a dream world, maybe. If word got out about me, I'd spend the rest of my life being stuck full of needles in some military laboratory."

"So how come it seems like I'm the only one in town who doesn't know about you."

"Not everyone knows—only the trustworthy ones."

"That's a bit harsh, isn't it? You must trust me now, otherwise you wouldn't be telling me all this."

Zero shrugged. "I don't know—*can* I trust you?"

His eyes were mesmerising as they fixed on hers. Just let me show you how much you can trust me, thought Candice. She leant in to kiss him, and he shied away.

And there it was. He *didn't* trust her, he *wasn't* attracted to her, in fact, judging by the look on his face, he must find her repulsive, and he had just made a big fat fool of her. She leapt to her feet, her face burning.

"Well, I think the whole thing is sick and perverted, and you've dragged my son into the middle of it. I'm going to put a stop to it."

"You wouldn't be the first person to threaten that," he said, shaking his head, "but you really, really don't want to go there..."

Candice barely heard him. "I'll go over Dave Bowman's head. I'll go to the media. I'll..."

Zero put out his bare hand and gently touched hers. It wasn't the re-straining grasp that she had been anticipating. Ever the pacifist, she thought, and started to pull away.

131

And fell to the ground, gasping for breath in the grip of unspeakable agony. It felt as if her ribs were being shattered one by one. A stabbing, bone deep pain worked its excruciating way down the length of her left forearm, and invisible flames were licking up both her legs. Zero looked down on her, but did not move to help. She heard him speak as if from a great distance.

"I said I don't suffer, but anyone who comes into skin contact with me does."

He crouched beside her and peered closely into her face. His eyes contained not a shred of pity.

"All the pain I should have experienced in my lifetime, transferred to you. I can't even begin to imagine what that must feel like."

She found her voice then, her scream echoing off the trees.

Sleeping With The Fishes

This poem won the Williamstown Literary Festival's Seagull Poetry Prize in 2009. The judges said that they were taken by the poem because it was "different". I suspect that, being a literary and not a genre festival, they were looking for the allegory in the piece; I didn't have the heart to tell them that there isn't one (or if there is, it only got in there by accident). Astute readers will find in "Sleeping With The Fishes" the partial origins of "Baptism". Any excuse to use the word "incarnadine"…

My wife lives in
our backyard pool.
Not her ideal
environment, but I try
to make her comfortable
by leaving it uncleaned;
she is shy, my wife, and she hides
from the neighbours
in the scummy green depths
of the deep end, concealed
beneath the leaf drifts.
On stormy nights,
she ventures to sit
on the steps,
cloud-dampened moonlight
turning her into
a figment of any casual

observer's imagination.
Dogs howl in harmony with
her inaudible song.
The wind whips
the water's surface
into a facsimile
of a choppy sea.
Her hair snaps behind her
like a banner,
revealing her perfect slime-slicked
breasts, and down each flank,
a row of pulsing,
incarnadine gills.

Hit Single

I come home to find Karla and her friends in my lounge preparing to shoot up.

"It's OK, Leo, it's not heroin," she says. "It's the latest thing–intravenous music. It's supposed to be the ultimate trip, and it's organic, so it's like, all natural. It's totally harmless." She looks up at me and deliberately widens her baby blue eyes, willing me to believe her.

"Intravenous music...what a crock of shit," I say.

"Fuck, man," says Jordan. "Why do you always have to be such a purist?" He almost spits out the last word, pronouncing it in the same tone he would use for 'Nazi baby killer'.

"How many times do I have to tell you, Karla, everything you put in your body affects you long term, one way or another," I say. "Everything."

Karla's expression turns sly. "That's not entirely true," she says. "You never did."

One of her friends sniggers. "That's brutal, dude." I reel back clutching at the invisible dagger she has plunged into my heart.

And she depresses the syringe into her vein.

* * *

Karla lives in my spare bedroom now. It's modified with soundproofing and padded walls especially for her. I know that I should turn her over to a state hospice, that I'm just being perverse, but this way I can make a liar of her. I *am* having an effect on her, a profound effect, in fact, as I'm currently the only thing standing between her and starvation.

The song radiates from every pore of her body, each limb broadcasting a different instrument, her torso providing a thumping bass line that beats in time with her heart. It was entrancing in the beginning, and I made a bit of money at first hiring her out to music festivals and rave parties until the novelty value wore off. Now I swear if I ever hear that

135

fucking song again I am going to kill myself, so I always wear noise-cancelling headphones when I go into her room.

Feeding her is a challenge, because she never stops dancing. I have learned to play the flute, and have become attuned to her steps, dancing with her as I position the end of the instrument between her lips and blow notes into her open mouth, all the while feeling like some kind of fucked-up Pied Piper.

It's easier to let her go naked. The soles of her feet are stained blue with the flat notes and discordant tones that dribble down her legs, and several times a day I have to dart in and mop up around her.

And she never. Stops. Dancing.

Fridge Wars

Sunday 5pm

"Did you forget to pay the power bill again, Gary?"

"Um...I dunno. Yeah, maybe..."

"For fuck's sake, Gary, can't you do anything right?"

"If you don't like the way I do things, why don't you do it yourself?"

"Because I shouldn't have to do every-fucking-thing around here, that's why."

"I just took you away for the weekend, didn't I?"

"To Ballarat, Gary. You took me to fucking Ballarat to spend the weekend at your mate Steve's place. Trying to sleep on a fold-out couch in the lounge while you two get plastered in the kitchen is not exactly my idea of a romantic weekend away."

"Speaking of beer...I could do with one right now."

"Well, there's no use looking in the fridge, because even if there are any in there, they'll be warm because you FUCKING DIDN'T PAY THE POWER BILL!"

"I'll just have a look...holy crap! What crawled in there and died?"

"Shut the door, quick, shut it, you moron! God, that stinks. Right, that's it."

"What are you doing?"

"I'm calling Cheryl to see if I can stay with her for a few days until you get the power back on."

"Don't you mean, 'we'?"

"Cheryl hates your guts. You know that."

"But she puts up with me for your sake."

"Oh, alright. I'll ask her. But you'd better have the power reconnected by Tuesday. And I'm not cleaning out the fridge. It's all your fault, so you can clean it."

"Yeah, yeah, whatever."

* * *

137

It is warm in the fridge. The air inside is ripe and rich, its interior awash with a unique combination of rotting organic matter. Week old pizza is slowly becoming one with its cardboard container. Slimy lettuce leaves merge with a furry zucchini. A long-forgotten bacon rasher turns iridescent with decay. A carton of milk bulges ominously. Had the jar of jam been properly sealed, it might have been immune, but not only has the lid been left loose, but the jar has tipped on its side, its contents oozing out as if it is bleeding.

And then there is light. It is dim and diffuse, and only illuminates the fridge contents for a second or two, but it is enough. The door shuts, and new life begins.

* * *

Sunday 8pm

"I can't believe I had to drive you all the way back here to pick up your wallet. Not that there's anything in it, I bet."

"I told you, Gillian - my Metrocard is in it, which is why I couldn't catch the train. I'm going to need that to get to work tomorrow, since you've made it very clear you won't drive me to work."

"Why should I? Cheryl reckons all that stuff you say about reducing your carbon footprint is a bullshit excuse for being too much of a loser to buy your own car. Anyway, I'd have to get up half an hour earlier to get us both to work on time. "

"Yeah, 'cos you need all the beauty sleep you can get..."

"What? I didn't hear what you said."

"Nothing—just talking to myself. Now, where did I leave my wallet...oh, here it is."

"About bloody time. I want to get back to Cheryl's in time to watch Rove."

"Didn't you want me to clean out the fridge?"

"Not now, dickhead! You'll have to come back tomorrow."

* * *

Life is simple at first in Fridgeworld, but as the first cells divide and multiply, they quickly mutate to form more complex organisms. The creatures in the vegetable drawer soon exhaust their food supply. Some of them grow wings to carry them up into the higher reaches of their world, thus granting them a reprieve from extinction. The microscopic monsters spawned by the jam have ferocious appetites, and develop needle-like appendages ideal for sucking the sugars from their prey. The first sour milk-dwelling animal to sprout a flagellum is irresistibly attractive to other milkfish, and soon they all bristle with whip-like limbs, navigating easily through their soupy sea. The decomposing pizza is a treasure trove of nutrients, a magnet for browsers, scavengers and predators alike. It gives birth to huge, shambling beasts that would be visible to the naked human eye, were anyone to gaze upon them.

They all co-exist in mindless harmony, eating, sleeping, breeding and dying—until a vegebat and a jamtiger find themselves reaching for the same scrap of mouldy cheese. The vegebat is quicker, and has the obvious advantage of aerial flight. But the jamtiger has two fiendishly sharp weapons protruding from its face, and is the more aggressive of the two. It seems like they are too evenly matched for the conflict to result in anything other than a stalemate.

Then the jamtiger's front paw closes on a projectile. It draws back its limb and throws. The vegebat, struck in the head, spirals lifeless to the ground. The jamtiger abandons the cheese, finding a much richer meal its foe. Hitherto unused synapses fire in its miniscule brain. Later, it breeds, and its offspring share its aptitude for conflict and domination.

It has invented war.

* * *

Monday 3.30 pm

"Hello, Steve? It's Gary... Yeah, yeah, nah, good, thanks. Well, no. Not really. I've split up with Gillian. It was kind of mutual... Yeah, you're right, she kicked me out. Usual bullshit—you never have any money, blah, blah, blah, you don't have any ambition, blah, blah, blah, you're always hitting on my friends, blah, blah, blah... No, I only did it once, and I was really drunk at the time... Yeah, Cheryl, the one with the big tits...

"Anyway, I was wondering if you could put me up for a while until I get my shit together... Nah, I've chucked it in, mate. Walked out this arvo. I always hated that job, anyway. Only took it on 'cos Gills was on my case... Yeah, I know, she hates being called Gills. I'm going to call her that all the time now. Gills, Gills, Gills, Gills, Gills... I'm at the flat now, mate. Borrowed my mum's car so I can pick up my things. Thought I'd get in while she's at work and take some of the good stuff. Is there anything you want?... Stereo, yep, yep, I was going to grab that... Flat screen TV, for sure...

"Fridge? Nah, mate, that won't fit in the car. Anyway, the power's been off here for a few days, and it was pretty rank last time I looked. Gills wanted me to clean it, but that ain't gonna happen... Yeah, mate, the shit in there's probably grown legs and walked off by itself by now.

"So I'll see you around 6 o'clock?... Cheers, mate. You're the best."

* * *

The other creatures in Fridgeworld are quick to develop defences against the jamtigers, but the jamtigers are even quicker on the offence, finding it more efficient to make the appropriate tools than to adapt their bodies. First to go are the milkfish, dredged out of their sea in nets and devoured in their thousands. Some milkfish grow sharp teeth to cut through the nets, and some come to prefer the lower reaches of the sour milk sea where the nets don't reach, but it is too little, too late. Their numbers dwindle below the critical level for survival.

When the last milkfish dies, it gives the jamtigers a good excuse to tear apart the milk carton and use it to fashion more elaborate weapons. The pizza mammoths are next in their sights. The massive animals take up a lot of space and use a lot of resources, both of which the jamtigers consider would be better put to use supporting themselves. Try as they might, the pizza mammoths cannot grow hide thick enough to withstand the jamtigers' arrows. When the last pizza mammoth falls, it is a cause for great celebration in Jamtiger Town.

Which leaves their oldest, most resourceful opponent, the vegebats. They come at the jamtigers on crystalline wings, their fragile bodies sheathed in almost impenetrable armour. Their weapons are made from chiselled fragments of peach pit, and their bombing campaign sends the jamtigers scrabbling to build adequate defenses. The leader of the jamtigers orders its team of scientists to be moved to a bunker in the depths of the pizza crust. Shielded from the attacking vegebats, they work tirelessly in their bid to invent the ultimate weapon, one that will wipe out the vegebats once and for all. And just when it the battle is just about to tip irrevocably in the vegebats' favour, one scientist has a Eureka moment. Clacking its face needles together in excitement, it describes its invention to the others. They work as one, constructing a complex series of levers and pulleys and barely contained lethal chemicals that stretches from the bunker to the surface. The jamtiger leader has the honour of flipping the switch.

But they have made a fatal error. In their eagerness to destroy the enemy, they failed to take account of the effect it would have on their own species. The chain reaction, once initiated, is swift and irreversible. Both vegebats and jamtigers pause, mid-battle, to shield their eyes from the blinding light. It is the last thing they will ever do, as all life and substance in Fridgeworld is obliterated.

* * *

Tuesday 5.15 pm

"Thanks again, Cheryl, for coming to help. The sooner I move out of here, the sooner I can get my bond back."

"Doesn't look like there's much left to move, Gills."

"What the...that prick! That fucking bastard! He took the T.V! And the stereo! I paid for those!"

"Calm down, Gills, calm down. We know where he's staying. We'll take T.J. and Carl and go up there on the weekend to get your stuff back."

"That's if he hasn't sold it already. Anyway, I'm not taking Carl. I don't want Gary to know I've got a new boyfriend already."

"You mean, you don't want him to put two and two together and figure out that you'd been screwing Carl for weeks before you broke up with him."

"Yeah, yeah, alright. Jeez, I thought you were meant to be on my side."

"The fridge is still here. You'll be able to put Carl to use moving that, at least."

"Ew, don't open it, Cheryl. The power's been off for ages, and it's full of rotting food."

"Gotta do it some time. I'll just take a quick peek...looks fine to me. Spotless, in fact. It's got a funny chemical smell, but otherwise it's fine."

"What? That can't be right...well, would you look at that. Gary must have cleaned it before he left. Wonders will never cease."

Tastes Like Chicken

The recipe
calls for breast
but I use
dark, fatty
thigh
It's cheaper
less prone
to overcooking
I slice it
dice it
spice it
and serve it
to my family
Blood pools
on the kitchen floor
I will limp for a while
but no matter
the flesh
will grow back
The kids say,
"Eww, gross!
I'm not eating that!"
They partake only
of the body
of Britney Spears

Marked

Hannah knew Silver wasn't right in the head from the moment he first came into the café.

Within seconds of taking his seat, he leaned across the counter and introduced himself to her in a high-pitched, reedy Irish lilt. Not the done thing, thought Hannah. Not the done thing at all. And he smelt funny; he gave off a distinct odour of smoke, with faint undertones of scorched flesh, cinnamon and pond scum. She gave his outstretched hand a perfunctory shake and went back to wiping down the counter. Usually customers would do a double-take at the sight of her face and then let their glance slide away, settling on a point somewhere just over her shoulder, but he stared, for a full minute, and then asked, without apology or preamble, "How did you get that?"

Oh, please, she thought. Not another creepy middle-aged scar fetishist. Her fingers flickered self-consciously over the thick, ropy red scar that started at her left temple, crossed her cheek, and wound down over her chin and neck before disappearing out of sight under the collar of her shirt.

"Lightning strike," she said. "Are you going to order something or what?"

Silver nodded as if he met lightning strike victims on a daily basis. "I've got a scar too," he said. "Do you want to see it?" Without waiting for an answer, he pulled open the grimy striped scarf around his neck to reveal a pale puckering of skin in the hollow of his throat. "And yes, I'd like a coffee, please. Black. Five sugars. How far down does it go?"

"What?" Hannah frowned and stopped in mid-pour.

"Your scar. How far down does it go?"

"All the way to my right foot. That's why I walk with a limp." He was starting to piss her off now.

"That must have hurt."

"I don't really remember. It happened fifteen years ago. I was only four."

Silver was still staring at her, his eyes glittering in his thin homely face. "Like being touched by the hand of God," he said dreamily. "Can I touch it?" He reached a hand out to her chest.

"No!" she said, slapping his hand away. He sat back in his chair, looking so much like a wounded puppy that she felt an unwelcome pang of guilt. "Here's your coffee," she said, slopping the cup across the counter. "I've got to go – it's the end of my shift."

* * *

He turned up nearly every day after that. He never mentioned Hannah's scar again, but he talked a lot about his own scar, each day telling a different story. One day he said he got it in a motorcycle accident. Another day he said he sustained it from the injuries that ended his career as a professional boxer. Taking in his gangly frame, Hannah greeted this with barely concealed scepticism. Despite his apparent lack of employment, he had an endless supply of bicycles, parking a different colour and model each day outside the café. Hannah suspected that he supported himself through petty thievery, but as long as he paid for his coffee and kept his hands off her stuff, she didn't much care. After a while she became used to his harmless brand of madness, and they settled into a routine of sorts, Silver holding a random one-way conversation between sips of coffee and Hannah doing her best to ignore him.

When he didn't show up for over a week, Hannah started to worry. Although he had told her several different versions of his life story, she realised that she knew virtually nothing about him. If something had happened to him, she didn't know if he had any close friends or family who could help out. And she didn't know his address, his phone number, or even his last name to check on him herself. So when he stepped out from behind a minivan as she was crossing the deserted car park at the end of a late shift, she didn't know whether to be frightened, angry or relieved.

"Jesus, Silver!" she said, punching him on the arm. "You nearly scared the shit out of me!"

"Hannah," he said, "I've got to show you something." He took hold of her elbow in a surprisingly powerful grip and propelled her towards the shadows of an alleyway on the far side of the car park. His customary loopy smile had disappeared, replaced with a grim frown of concentration that etched deep lines into his face. Hannah eyed the alleyway ahead. Her heart beat faster in trepidation and she fought in vain to free herself from his grasp. A police siren wailed a few streets away, and Hannah looked around hopefully, but it faded into the distance.

"Are you on something?" she said, struggling to keep up with his long-legged stride. "Come on, Silver, stop mucking around and let me go."

He stopped at the entrance to the alleyway, raised his finger to his lips to indicate silence, and pointed. Hannah looked and saw a tiny child, clad only in a nappy, rummaging around in the overflow of rubbish from a skip bin. She looked to be barely two years old, with tight blonde curls framing a cherubic face. Silver darted forward and grabbed the girl by the hair, holding her out at arm's length. Hannah tensed in expectation of the scream that was certain to follow, but the girl remained silent, her contorted face the only clue to the pain she must be feeling.

Silver gave the child a vicious shake. "Do you see, Hannah?" he said. The child wriggled and squirmed, tears spilling down her cheeks. "Do you see?"

"What are you talking about, you fucking lunatic?" sobbed Hannah. "Let her go!" She grabbed the child and yanked her away from Silver, leaving him standing with a fistful of the little girl's hair.

"Poor little baby," she crooned, hugging the girl close and turning her back on Silver. "I won't let the bad man hurt you."

Hannah looked down at the child in her arms and gasped. Suddenly, she did see. The girl's face had gone slack and expressionless. Beneath her now translucent skin, a dark, grimacing monster pulsed and stirred.

* * *

Silver caught the girl as she fell from Hannah's nerveless arms, bundled her into a sleeping bag and slung her over her shoulder like a pig in a sack. Numbly obedient, Hannah followed him down a labyrinth of dimly lit streets to a small workshop in a light industrial area. He unlocked a side door and ushered her in.

The inside of the workshop was immaculate. Blue gingham curtains decorated the windows. A vase full of daisies sat next to a folded newspaper in the centre of a red Formica-topped table. Half a dozen bicycles in various stages of repair rested against one wall. An adjacent wall was taken up with a huge furnace. Its interior was ablaze.

Silver motioned her to sit on a camp stretcher. He dropped the sleeping bag on the floor and kicked it closer to the furnace. He picked up a four foot long metal pike, its tip sheathed in what looked like gold. Despite the oppressive heat in the room, Hannah hugged herself tightly and shivered.

Without warning, Silver opened the furnace door, reached into the bag and pulled out the child by the foot. He flung her into the flames. Hannah screamed. The child's skin blackened and shrivelled almost instantly. Hannah's scream became a whisper of pure distilled terror as the creature within emerged as if from an obscene chrysalis.

It perched toad-like on the lip of the furnace door, its lumpy bruise-purple skin impervious to the heat. Red slanted eyes glared from the sides of its hairless misshapen head. Two vertical slits sufficed as nostrils. Thin crooked fangs crowded its wide lipless mouth. Each bony hand and foot had four digits ending in curved yellow talons.

The creature tensed its haunches as it prepared to spring at Silver. Before it could leap, he skewered it through the chest with the pike. It writhed on the end of the pike for a moment before slumping to the ground. Hannah gagged as it dissolved into a puddle of putrid ooze which rapidly evaporated, leaving behind a cloying smell of cinnamon. Within minutes, there was no trace of either child or monster.

Silver shook off his overcoat, hung it over the back of a chair and sat next to Hannah. His hair stuck to his forehead with sweat and he was trembling slightly from his exertions. All the menace that had exuded from him in the alleyway was gone.

"What *was* that thing?" asked Hannah.

"A Voraku," said Silver. "A manifestation of malevolent energy that takes possession of human form by invading the bodies of very young children. The child that you saw was only a shell. The way I found it wandering around at night alone like that, it must have recently killed its host parents. I've been keeping them at bay for years, but there's been a sudden upswing in their numbers, and I'm starting to lose the battle."

"If these monsters are possessing children and killing the parents, how come it isn't all through the news?"

"It is." He picked the newspaper up off the table and tossed it to her. "Dozens Dead From Spate Of Arsons", the front page headline claimed. "Of course, the cops don't know the truth of it. They'd think I was crazy if I tried to explain it to them."

"They're not the only ones," muttered Hannah.

"I can't do it on my own," said Silver. "I need to find more people who have the ability to see through Voraku disguises. Like you. You're Marked, Hannah." He gestured at her scar, and she flinched away from him.

"No," she said. She stood and crossed to the door. "No, no, no. I don't care what I've seen, or think I've seen tonight. I am not about to start bumping off little kids. Stay away from me, or so help me, I'll go to the cops myself." The chill night air blasted her as she opened the door and hobbled away. Silver didn't pursue her, but his parting words stung as he shouted after her.

"But you're Marked, Hannah. You're Marked..."

* * *

Two weeks later, Hannah retraced her steps to Silver's workshop. She knocked on the door. Silver opened it almost immediately and let her in. He looked much smaller by day, almost harmless, thought Hannah. She lowered her backpack to the floor and slumped at the table.

"You bastard, Silver," she said wearily. "Ever since you showed me that thing, I can't stop thinking about it. I can hardly sleep, and when I do, I have nightmares. If I get one more warning at work, I'm going to get fired. And I...I saw another one. I didn't just see another Voraku; I saw it take over a child. It was a little boy, maybe eighteen months old, and he was playing in the park. He chased a ball into some bushes, and this mist rose up and just sort of soaked into him. I don't know how to describe it exactly, but it was as if the mist hollowed him out from the inside." She looked to Silver for confirmation.

"Did you puke?" he said. "I did the first time I saw it."

She gave a small, hysterical giggle. "Yeah, I puked."

"And then what did you do?"

"What else could I do?" She bent and opened the top of her backpack. A dark-haired toddler stared impassively up at them. His face was the only part of him that was clearly visible, the rest being obscured beneath knotted lengths of rope that encircled his body. "I didn't want him wriggling around in there," Hannah explained. "Lucky his babysitter was too busy sucking face with her boyfriend," she said, sounding anything but lucky, "or I might not have got away with it."

Silver sighed and looked down at the floor. When he looked up, his eyes were brimming with tears. "Are you ready for this?" he said.

She shook her head. "Will I ever be?"

She opened the furnace door and threw the child into the fire.

The Blue Screen of Death

Three days later it happened again. Sara woke up and found herself dead.

Her soul bobbed against the ceiling as she looked down at her body, half-tangled in the bed sheets. An exquisite dark-skinned creature hovered at her side, his wings barely stirring the air.

"Azrael!" she said. "We've got to stop meeting like this. Did you get the right day this time?"

"Um...no. Sorry. Another false alarm. It's this new software."

Azrael flicked his glossy black ringlets out of his eyes and bent over his Pocket PC, stabbing viciously at it with a golden stylus.

"Bloody Microsoft!" he said. "OK, I think I've got it now. All things going to plan, I shouldn't be seeing you again for around another fifty years."

"That's if I don't turn into an axe-murderer or something in the meantime," said Sara.

The angel laughed. "That's not about to happen. You know all that stuff about free will? Complete bollocks. You couldn't be bad if you tried."

He gave the Pocket PC a few more prods. It chimed in assent. He smiled and waved cheerily as her soul plunged into a swirling vortex and jolted back into her body.

* * *

Sara died again later in the week. She was having dinner at her parents' home when her soul slipped out, leaving her body slumped in the gravy. Her mother screamed hysterically and dragged Sara's body to the floor. She threw all of her considerable weight into thumping on Sara's chest, in what Sara could only assume was an attempt at CPR. Azrael shook his head at the performance.

150

"You'll probably have a few cracked ribs from that," he said. "Look, I could just take you now, if you like. You're going to end up in Heaven anyway, so what difference does it make?"

"Thank you, no," Sara said hastily. "Can't God fix your computing system? He is meant to be omnipotent, isn't he?"

Azrael blushed. "The thing is...he's on holiday."

"On holiday? God's on *holiday*? How long for?"

"Oh, not long. Just a hundred years or so."

"Well... don't you have any computer experts in Heaven who can take a look at it?"

"There's a few good ones up there, but no *good* ones, if you know what I mean."

"My brother is a...I mean, he's pretty clued up on computers. I could ask him to take a look at it."

Azrael shook his head. "He'd have to die and go to Heaven before I could let him have access to the system. Which means we have two problems. It's not his time to die, and when it is, he won't be going to Heaven."

Sara sighed. "I'm not surprised."

"Come on," Azrael said. "Time to send you back. Third time lucky?"

"I didn't know angels believed in luck," Sara started to say, before she landed with a thump back in her body.

* * *

That Sunday after church, Sara paid an impromptu visit to her brother Cliff. She picked her way past overflowing wheelie bins and banged on the door to his flat. After a minute he opened the door, dressed only in a greying pair of boxer shorts. He blinked and squinted in the sunlight.

"What time is it?" he rasped.

Sara checked her watch. "1.30," she said.

"Shit," he said. "I hate it when I'm woken up early."

He opened the door wider and ushered Sara inside. She breathed as shallowly as she could. Cliff's flat had a distinctive smell, of stale smoke, foot odour, mildew and grease, the latter coming from the takeaway bar next door.

Cliff found himself a T-shirt and a cigarette while Sara cleared a space on the couch.

"Mum told me about your little episode the other night," he said. "What was that all about?"

Sara told him. Cliff blew smoke rings towards the stained ceiling.

"Yeah," he said, "I bet I know what the problem is with their system."

Sara nodded. "I thought you might. I also thought that, seeing as you're a hacker who is talented enough to be wanted in seven different countries, you might be able to get into Heaven's system and fix it for me."

"I don't know, Sara," said Cliff. "Technically, I'm more of a cracker than a hacker. I could probably get in – I *am* that good – but it doesn't sound right somehow. What kind of cracker breaks into a system and fixes it? It would be against the cracker's code – if there were a cracker's code, that is."

"There's one thing I forgot to tell you," said Sara. "You're not in Heaven's database."

"But if I got into the system," Cliff said, "I could add my name. And give myself a Methuselah-sized lifespan while I was at it."

"That's if the Devil doesn't claim you first."

"No problem. I'll hack into Hell's system too."

* * *

Cliff rang Sara a few days later.

"Hi, sis," he said. "Job done. It was a piece of piss getting in – those angels are so trusting, their system doesn't have any protection. Oh, by the way, I'm calling from the hospital. Would you be able to pick me up? And I need a place to stay and some cash. I had a little fire at my place."

"What happened?" asked Sara. "It couldn't have been a vengeful bolt of lightning from God. He's still on holiday."

"Well, like I said, it was easy getting into Heaven…but the firewall on Hell's system is something else…"

Hell Is Other People

I got the idea from the fisherman. The nun inside me is dead against it, and as usual, she is making a lot of noise about it. No one outside of my body can hear her. But even although it hurts me more than it hurts her, I deliver her a psychic slap to shut her up. I want to get this exactly right, and so does the fisherman. It's purely a matter of professional pride for him—in true conflicted human fashion, he is one part fascinated and nine parts appalled.

I've spent hours fashioning the bait into the right configuration. Now I extrude it from my greater mass and huddle down, concealed beneath heaps of refuse. Then I make it wail.

The fisherman assured me that this ploy would draw someone to me like no other bait could, and a quick trawl through the other consciousnesses in me found concurrence. Sure enough, the lid of the dumpster soon opens. It is night outside, and I can barely discern the features of the face peering in. I catch a glimpse of facial hair—male, then—and he is reaching in, just as predicted, to pick up what he thinks is a naked human baby.

I let out a thin tendril of flesh, allowing him to raise the 'infant' to his chest. He holds it close, patting it gently on the back, and tries to wrap his coat around it to shield it from the cold. That's when he notices the line.

It's too late. He's hooked. I send tiny needles of matter burrowing into his flesh. They penetrate his tongue and throat first, choking off all sound. Oh, he will scream alright, when he realises what has happened to him. I feel a little bad about that, thanks to the nun. She has taught me the meaning of guilt.

But a being's gotta eat, right?

I get the first taste of his psyche. The fisherman was wrong—he did not pick up a child out of a sense of pity or civic duty or any other supposedly noble motivation. He did it out of lust. Oh, the things he intended to do to that baby...in amongst my victim's fear and pain and panic is a sense of resignation. He thinks he had it coming, apparently, and believes that his absorption is some kind of divine retribution for his sins.

I laugh. I learnt about irony from the prostitute, who possesses a far more lively intelligence than those of her profession are commonly credited with. She is not going to like this new guy.

In fact, I think all my dinners are going to give him hell.

Dark Wing

Leta shifted restlessly in her saddle. They were less than an hour's ride from the town of Borderlee, and from one of her favourite inns. After nearly three weeks in the field, she longed for a soft mattress, a home-cooked meal and a tankard or two of ale. And if she threw in a few extra coins, she could soak away three weeks' worth of grime in a tub of steaming warm water up to her chin. With soap, no less! She glanced round at her companions and wrinkled her nose. Now if she could only persuade the rest of them to take a bath...

She was shaken from her reverie by the sound of pounding hooves. A sweat-lathered horse rounded the corner in front of them and reared up as its rider pulled it to a sudden stop. The rider, a slightly built young man, slid from the horse's back. "You're mercenaries, aren't you?" he gasped. "Do you have a Healer?"

Zak, the leader of the twelve-strong band, nodded.

"It's my wife," said the young man. "She needs a Healer, urgently. Please...I'll pay..." He fumbled with a purse at his belt.

"It's up to our Healer," Zak said calmly. He craned over his shoulder and looked at Leta. "Mother?"

Leta sighed. It looked like that bath would have to wait a little longer. "Of course," she said. "Lead the way. Zak, I'll meet you at Borderlee when I'm finished." She noted with a frown the way the distressed young man flinched at the name of the town.

"Thank you," said the young man, his relief palpable. "Our home is only ten minutes' ride from here. I pray that it is time enough." He sprung on to his horse's back. Leta nudged her mount with her heels and turned it to follow him.

"Nim, you go with her," said Zak.

Leta chewed nervously at her lip. Before Nim had joined them, she would have welcomed the company of another woman in the band. But the huge tawny-skinned Kamankayan had an uncanny knack for making her feel weak and inadequate. Then again, she had the same effect on most men as well.

The young man stared at Nim as she reined her horse out of line. The intricate lineage tattoo inscribed on her left cheek intensified her fearsome appearance, but he said nothing as he urged his horse into a gallop, beckoning over his shoulder for Leta and Nim to follow.

His home was a tiny thatch-roofed cottage perched on the edge of a small glade of trees. Leta blinked as her eyes adjusted to the gloom inside the single room of the cottage. It was sparsely furnished, with just a table and two chairs, a few food-encrusted pots and plates by the hearth, and a large straw-stuffed mattress in the far corner, set on the bare earth floor. A young woman lay on her back on the mattress, her belly bulging above her. Blood soaked into the already filthy fabric under her hips. She lifted her head from the mattress, fear and pain etched into her face. "Feo?" she whispered.

He rushed to her side and dropped to his knees, stroking her forehead. "It's going to be alright, Ani," he said. I've brought someone who can help you."

"How long has she been in labour?" said Leta.

"Two days," said Feo. "I don't think she can take much more."

Leta's heart sank. "I'm not a midwife. I deal with knife wounds and arrow piercings and the occasional lame horse. Why didn't you fetch the midwife from Borderlee?"

"I was on my way there, but I came across you first. I thought any Healer was better than none." His eyes slid sideways, avoiding hers.

"And?"

"What do you mean?"

"And what's the real reason you didn't want to ride on to Borderlee?" Leta stepped closer to Ani. Even sweat soaked and drawn with exhaustion, the young woman was a beauty. Leta drew in a sharp breath as she saw for the first time that she was bound, with two stout ropes encircling her wrists at one end and tethered to solid metal rings imbedded in the wall.

"My wife claims that I am not the father of the baby," Feo said, almost too low for Leta to hear. "We are—were–from Borderlee, and she told anyone who would listen that she was ravished by a...a demon. Half the townsfolk didn't believe her and said she was mad, and the other half did believe her and said she was cursed. Either way, we had to leave. I doubt the midwife would have come. She was one of the believers."

"That doesn't explain why she is tied up," said Nim. She scowled at Feo, her hand hovering dangerously close to the dagger at her waist.

"It was for her own good," he explained. "She kept trying to kill herself."

Suddenly Ani shrieked and arched her back, her arms straining as she fought the ropes. "It hurts, it hurts!"

"There, there, sweetheart, everything's going to be alright," Leta said, just as she would to soothe an injured horse. "Nim, will you go and get my provisions outside?" Nim swiftly complied. Leta rummaged through her bulging saddle bag, tossing aside half-chewed strips of jerky, items of soiled clothing and assorted needles and thread before finding a small vial. She uncorked it and tipped a few drops of the contents into Ani's mouth. Ani's cries subsided to a soft whimper.

"I don't know how you can work with that mess," said Nim. She picked up a long length of plaited leather cord with a small weighted ball on each end. "Oh, look, here's your bola. Weren't you looking for that the other day?"

"Please excuse my friend Nim," Leta said to Feo. "She's Kamankayan–they're not known for their tact." She shot a pointed glance at Nim, who retired, grinning, to a corner of the room. Leta returned her attention to the stricken woman. She ran her hands through her short-cropped grey hair as she considered her options. Ani trembled, her eyes rolling in her head like a terrified animal.

Like an animal...

"Get her up," said Leta. "You'll have to cut her loose and get her up. Standing, on all fours, it doesn't matter, as long as she's not on her back."

Feo hesitated. With an impatient snort, Nim strode over to Ani. She drew her sword and severed the ropes with one stroke. Hooking her arms under Ani's, she hoisted her into an upright position. Ani's head lolled on her chest and her bare feet dangled, barely touching the ground. "Will this do?" said Nim. Feo took Ani's hand in his and gripped it tightly.

Leta squatted and peered up between Ani's sodden skirts. She smiled. "That will do nicely," she said.

Ani lifted her head, her entire body tense, and groaned, a long, low guttural sound that sent chills down Leta's spine. "Good girl, Ani," she urged. "One more push, and..."

With a splash of bloody fluids, the baby slid from Ani's body into Leta's waiting hands. "It's a girl!" said Leta. With that pronouncement, the infant began to wail. "Well, we know she has good healthy lungs," she said, smiling up at the new parents. "Ten fingers, ten toes..." Gently she turned the baby on to its stomach. She stared, speechless with horror.

"...and two perfect little black wings," concluded Nim.

Ani wept helplessly, the baby still tethered to her body by the umbilical cord, and sagged into Feo's arms. "Take it away," she sobbed. "I don't even want to look at it. Take it away!"

* * *

Leta had not dared to take the malformed baby into Borderlee, so she had waited in the woods just outside the town for Nim to fetch her son Zak from the inn. "I'm taking the baby to the Sisterhood of Yana," said Leta. "They have an orphanage a couple of days' ride from here. A day and a half, if we sleep little and ride hard." She looked at the baby, who slept swaddled in her arms. "Which we will have to do if there is any hope for her survival. She won't last long without milk, but the Sisterhood will have wet nurses." As if reacting to the words, the baby stirred and woke, crying lustily. Nim took her from Leta's arms and cradled her awkwardly, crooning a Kamankayan lullaby to her in a surprisingly melodic contralto.

"How can you be sure they will take her?" said Zak. "An abomination like that..." He trailed off, the sad alternative hanging unspoken between them. Leta smiled grimly. "The credo of Yana is 'Compassion for All'. They specialize in abominations."

"By the way," said Nim, "we can't keep calling her 'abomination'. How about 'Caris'? I had a hunting falcon once named Caris." She put the tip of her little finger into the baby's mouth to pacify her, then jerked it away with a muttered curse. "I pity the poor wet nurse who has to feed this one." She held up her finger, now welling with blood from two tiny punctures. "Caris has teeth."

Zak sidled away, one eye on the baby as if it might fly up out of Nim's arms and latch onto his neck. "I suppose we can do without you for a few days," he said. "We've just picked up a job escorting a merchant caravan. It should be routine. We'll meet you back at Illac." He looked at Nim. "I know, I know," said Nim. " 'Go with her.' "

* * *

"I'm getting too old for this," Leta grumbled as she rubbed grit from her eyes and mounted her horse. Nim had set a blistering pace, riding through the night and prodding Leta awake after only a few hours' sleep. At least the baby had been quiet, she thought. Caris gazed solemnly up at her from her makeshift sling across Leta's chest. Leta gazed back. She would be such a pretty wee thing, she thought, if it wasn't for those wings.

They made good time throughout the day. As the shadows lengthened toward sunset, the road dwindled to a narrow path and wound gradually upward. They stopped on the edge of a dense forest. Leta pointed at a distant clearing just visible over the tops of the trees. "That's where we are heading," she said.

"If we keep going, we could be there by morning," said Nim.

"Do you think we could eat first?" Leta fought to keep the petulant tone from her voice.

"You civilians–always thinking of your stomachs," said Nim. But she dismounted and set off into the woods for firewood while Leta settled the sleeping baby into a makeshift nest in the roots of a young oak.

Caris was the first to hear it. She woke screaming in a staccato, high-pitched warble that seemed to echo off the trees. A heartbeat later, Leta heard a deep thrumming sound, like a harnessed tornado, cutting through the child's cries. Her cloak fluttered about her in a sudden breeze. The horses reared and whinnied in panic, threatening to break their tethers. A violent gust of wind pressed down on Leta's back, and she looked up.

The creature bearing down from the skies might have been beautiful, had it not been for the undiluted expression of malice on his face. His glossy black hair hung in soft tendrils halfway down his back. His ebony wings spanned twice as wide as Nim was tall, casting a shadow on Leta and Caris, whose tiny face had turned red with screaming. His bare feet swept up an eddy of dust as he landed, gripping the earth with talon-like nails as long as Leta's forefinger. He was clad in only a loose-fitting loin cloth. A long hairless tail tipped in a vicious-looking barb coiled lazily around his thighs. Leta felt an insane urge to reach out and touch his heavily muscled bare chest.

"I have come for my child," he said.

Leta's head swam. Every particle of her being screamed at her that he was evil, yet her trembling legs moved of their own volition to, stepping aside to let him approach Caris. He picked up the screaming baby and roughly undressed her, examining her as if she were livestock. His alabaster face twisted with disgust.

"She is useless," he spat. "Too human by far. She must be culled."

Leta shook her head like a dog shaking off fleas. Through sheer force of will, she fought through the fog of enchantment the demon was casting on her. "You'll not harm her," she said, "not while I have breath in my body."

He smiled, reached out a finger and caressed her chin in a gesture that was both tender and menacing. Her flesh tingled where he touched her. "Little human," he said, "do not tempt me." He struck her across the face, sending her reeling to the ground. Caris's cries were abruptly choked off as he covered her nose and mouth with his palm. Leta saw a blur of movement out of the corner of her eye and heard the hiss of a sword drawn from a scabbard. Nim now stood in the demon's path, her sword tip aimed unwaveringly at his throat.

"Nice wings," said Nim. "I reckon I could make a new jerkin and pair of boots out of them."

With an outraged roar, the demon dropped Caris and took to the air. Leta rolled to catch her before she hit the ground, shielding her with her body as Nim and the demon fought. Nim's weapon was a blur over her head as she warded off the demon's frenzied attack. Although he lacked Nim's skill and finesse, it was obvious that his strength and aerial position gave him a distinct advantage. His tail lashed out again and again, slicing into her face and shoulders as she ducked and crouched.

Leta sobbed as she cowered over Caris, determined to defend her even although it seemed futile. If only there was some way to help Nim... but Leta was no fighter. The only kills she'd ever scored were rabbits and game birds with the bola she had wielded since childhood.

Leta stared trancelike for a moment at the demon's massive beating wings as a desperate plan formed in her mind. It was a long shot, but it just might work. Her bag had fallen open an arm's reach from her, disgorging its contents on the ground. Still with her eyes fixed on the demon, she picked up her bola, stood, and began to swing it over her head. The bola whirred through the air, all but inaudible over the sounds of battle. She took aim and let it go.

The demon heard the whistle of the balls flying to meet him. He disengaged from Nim and rose in the air, half-turning towards Leta, but she had expected this, and the bola struck true, entangling itself about the demon's beating wings. He howled in pain and fury and plummeted to the ground at Nim's feet. With preternatural speed, Nim swung her sword and neatly decapitated him.

Shakily Leta approached Nim and examined her wounds. "I'd better get a salve on those scratches before you end up looking like that." She gestured at the grass beneath the demon's corpse, which was brown and shriveled from the black fluid oozing from its neck.

"Does this mean I won't be getting any more marriage proposals with these scars?" said Nim dryly. "More importantly, we need to get that carcass buried before it poisons some poor unsuspecting scavenging animal. "And I wasn't joking about making a new jerkin out of those wings–that is, if you don't want them. After all, you brought him down."

Leta shuddered. "Take them," she said. "I don't need any reminders of this day. I'll have my nightmares for that."

* * *

Leta's head was nodding with fatigue when they plodded into the courtyard of the orphanage the next morning, but she was not too exhausted to notice the eight foot tall wooden poles flanking the gateway. The complex pattern of circles and spirals chiseled into them seemed to meld seamlessly with the grain of the exotic-looking dark wood. Her horse shied a little, its ears pricked up and nostrils flaring as they rode past the poles, and she felt a strange tingling sensation.

Then it was gone, her senses overtaken by the sights and sounds of children at play. A small golden-haired girl ran nimbly in front of Leta's horse, her foxy, fur-covered face beaming with glee. An older boy followed, moving almost as swiftly despite having to drag his grotesquely twisted right foot behind him. In the shade of a tree, a young Sister dressed in sage green robes played catch with a girl only a few years younger than herself. The younger girl's eyes were pupil-less milky white orbs. She stood with her head turned side-on to the Sister and caught the ball unerringly each time by listening for the silvery tinkle of the bell encased in the woven leather ball.

Another Sister helped them dismount and took their horses to a nearby stable, while a third escorted them to the quarters of the Abbess. Leta took her saddle bag with her. After what had happened, she was reluctant to be parted from it, even in this peaceful haven.

The head of the Sisterhood was a tall, spare woman about Leta's age with long ash blonde hair restrained in a single braid down her back. She introduced herself as Sister Salma, and served them herself from a platter of freshly baked oat cakes and cool pitchers of spiced wine. Between mouthfuls, Leta told her tale. Salma said little. At its conclusion, she took Caris from Leta's arms. Gently she probed Caris's mouth, counting her teeth, and then unwrapped her swaddling clothes. She stroked one leathery wing, her expression unreadable. "Please excuse me," she said. "There is something urgent I must attend to." She left the room, taking the baby with her.

Leta's mind was in turmoil. What if the Sisterhood refused to accept Caris? What if they, too, thought she was an abomination? What if they were drowning the defenseless infant right now while she sat here doing nothing? Just when she was about to go in search of Salma, she returned, with Caris tucked expertly in the crook of one arm and a bowl of a meaty-smelling broth in her other hand. She settled into her chair opposite Leta and spooned tiny mouthfuls into Caris's mouth, which she received greedily.

Nim leaned over and examined the bowl. "Ground beef?" she said. "For a newborn baby? I'm no expert on these things, but are you sure you know what you are doing?"

"Caris isn't the first of her kind to have been sheltered by the Sisterhood," she said. "Aside from her unusual eating habits, her needs are the same as any other child, human or otherwise. Love. Shelter. Acceptance. Protection."

Nim snorted. "No offence, Sister, but I'd like to see you lot protect her from one of those demon things that tried to take her."

Salma smiled enigmatically. "We have our methods."

"The gateway poles," said Leta. "They're talismans against evil. I felt them assessing me as we came through the gate."

Salma nodded. "Had your intentions been less than honourable, you would now both be piles of ash. And in case you're wondering, their protection extends over the entire orphanage. They're just as effective against an aerial attack."

"You mentioned that Caris isn't the first... winged child you have had here. What happened to the others?" said Leta.

Salma settled Caris into a crib in the corner of the room before answering. "There was only one other." She turned her back on them and slipped her robe off her shoulders. Each of Salma's shoulder blades was studded with a large black bony protrusion.

Leta gasped. "Someone cut off your wings."

Nim started out of her chair. "If you even think of harming that child..." she growled.

Salma lifted her hands in surrender. "This was done to me before I came to the Sisterhood. Thank the gods, you have spared Caris from a similar fate."

Unexpected tears welled in Leta's eyes, and she turned her head away from Nim, sure that the swordswoman would see them as a sign of weakness. For a brief moment she had considered adopting the baby herself, but life in a traveling mercenary band was no life at all for a child, let alone one like Caris.

"Before you go, I have something for you," said Salma. She crossed to a small cabinet mounted on the wall, and returned bearing two ebony amulets on leather thongs. She hung one around each of their necks. "The demon horde will be displeased that you have killed one of their own," she said. "These are carved from the same tree that gave us the gateway poles. They will lose potency the further you go from the source, but they will protect you at least until you are out of the demons' domain."

"And if they don't work," said Nim, "I've always got this." She patted the hilt of her sword.

Leta hugged her saddle bag to her chest. The bola felt reassuringly heavy in the bottom of the bag. "And this," she said.

* * *

Leta felt her amulet vibrate gently as they exited the gates. She felt a strange emptiness as they rode away, that went beyond the relief of setting down the burden of responsibility for baby Caris. Nim gave a backward glance at the orphanage.

"Babies," she said. "Lovely to hold, even lovelier to hand back." Leta caught her swiping her hand surreptitiously across her cheek. Leta smiled and leant over, punching Nim playfully in the arm.

"You big softie," she said.

Waking Down

A carotid artery
pulses
just below
the threshold
of movement.
A tongue trembles
and skitters
across skin.
Dawn comes grey
as a dead girl's eyes.

Crimes of Faith

Alec gave the dead bird at his feet a desultory kick, sending a small swarm of flies into orbit. A few feathers fell from its already sparse plumage. A small sign, handwritten on a torn piece of cardboard, was tied to the bird's limp neck. "GOD LOVER", it proclaimed in red lettering. Alec took a step back to escape the miasma of decay rising from the carcase.

"I don't get it," he said. "Why would somebody dump a dead turkey on my doorstep?"

Alec sensed his wife Emily tense beside him as Officer Mathers picked at a pimple on his chin. "I've seen this before," Mathers said. "It's the time of year. Apparently, Christians used to celebrate some significant day in December with feasting and gift-giving. Turkey was a traditional dish."

"I don't think this turkey's exactly fit for human consumption," said Alex. "And anyway, what's that got to do with us?"

"Whoever delivered this must think you're Christians. They take faith crimes very seriously around here, you know. We caught a Muslim family with a prayer mat stashed under their living room floorboards, and while they were in custody awaiting trial, their house burnt down." Mathers fixed Alec with what he presumed was the officer's attempt at a steely-eyed glare. "Have you given anyone reason to suspect you of a faith crime?"

Emily stepped forward, her hands clenched at her side. "Of course not! We're decent, tax-paying, law-abiding atheists, just like you. Whoever did this," she said, waving at the turkey and wrinkling her nose in disgust, "is the real criminal. They're probably Christians themselves, and are just trying to deflect suspicion onto someone else. Why else would they know so much about forbidden rituals? You should be out there right now tracking down those animals."

Alec put a restraining hand on her shoulder. "Please excuse my wife," he said. "She's been shaken quite badly by this, and we're both worried that next time it could be something worse than rotting poultry."

"Oh, I don't think anything else will come of this. If my suspicions are correct, then the perpetrator's bark is worse than his bite. Not that I can prove anything, of course," Mathers said, glancing at Emily, "so it's unlikely I'll be able to press charges, but I'll have a quiet word with a few people and put a stop to it." He took a business card from his pocket and handed it to Alec with a yellow-toothed smile. "If you have any further problems in the meantime, here's my direct line."

"Thank you, officer," said Alec. He gave Mathers a steely-eyed glare of his own. "I sincerely hope I won't need this."

* * *

"I still can't believe it," Emily said, shedding garments as she paced up and down the bedroom late that evening. "Why on earth would some-one think we were Christians?"

"You know how paranoid these small-town people can be of out-siders," said Alex. "Once we introduce ourselves properly and show them we're not toting crucifixes or swigging holy water, this will all blow over."

Emily scowled. "Just let me get my hands on whoever dumped that maggoty thing on my doorstep and I'll show them just how un-Christian I am."

Alec laughed and drew her into his embrace, his chin resting on the top of her head. "Did you know you're cute when you're angry?" Emily pouted and thumped him lightly in the chest. He glanced at his watch.

"We'd better hurry up, he said. "It's almost time." Quickly they fin-ished undressing, put on floor-length dark hooded robes, and de-scended the stairs into the basement. He fumbled in the dark for a mo-ment until he found the packet of matches in a concealed pocket in his robe. As he struck a match and touched it to the first of a line of can-dles, a shriek came from the far side of the room. Ignoring the noise, he continued down the line until he had lit all thirteen. He picked up a hunting knife with an ornately carved bone handle. The shrieks became louder, competing with the sound of steel scraping against steel as he sharpened the blade.

"Honey, could you do something about that noise?" he said to Emily. "I have to concentrate on getting the measurements on this pentagram right."

"Sure thing, sweetheart." Emily took a candle in each hand and entered the shadows of the basement. The shrieks were coming from a bound, gagged and naked teenaged girl who was tied spread eagled to a large stone-topped table. Her small breasts quivered as she struggled fruitlessly to free herself, her short auburn hair slicked close to her scalp with sweat. She stared imploringly as Emily positioned the candles at either side of the girl's head. Emily wrapped her fingers around the girl's windpipe, smiling over her shoulder at Alec as the girl's scream became a barely audible gurgle. "After the day we've had, this is just the therapy I need."

"You've got to admit," said Alec, "it is pretty funny. Fancy someone suspecting us of faith crimes."

Diagnosis

The man in the white coat waited until his audience's chatter subsided to an expectant hush.

"Good morning, ladies and gentlemen. I'm Dr Chad Goldsmith. You are here to witness a demonstration of a diagnostic tool that will revolutionize the health industry." He snapped his fingers. A woman stepped forward from the shadows to stand on a small dais next to him.

"This is Shellie," he said. "Isn't she a superb specimen?"

The audience nodded their assent. Dressed in a simple black crop top and leggings, her blonde hair swept back in a ponytail, Shellie stood tall and still, staring straight ahead with a faint beauty queen smile. Chad began to attach small adhesive pads to various points on her head and torso. The pads trailed wires to a large featureless metallic box.

"Can I direct your attention to the display," he said, indicating the five metre square screen on the wall behind him. Fifty-three heads obediently tilted up to view a series of horizontal bar graphs. "The Well-Mate provides the user with a comprehensive summary of his or her physical, mental and emotional health. This first series of graphs measures Shellie's nutritional needs, determined from an analysis of a urine sample and a pin prick blood sample. The procedure for collecting and analysing these samples takes only a few minutes and is simple enough for a layperson to complete. I had Shellie fast for twenty-four hours so we could show you some negative results. As you can see, she is getting low on several vitamins and minerals, and her protein and carbohydrate levels are edging into the red."

"This next screen shows her general health and fitness. Shellie is in the peak of physical condition – her blood pressure, cardiovascular fitness and muscular strength are all showing near-optimum levels. The WellMate detects no bacterial or viral infections. It can also give instant diagnosis of most common cancers. Again, for the purposes of this demonstration, I instructed Shellie to have only four hours' sleep last night, which is indicated here as a deficit."

"We move on now to Shellie's mental health. Today it is robust, as usual, except for her persistent mild phobia of large insects. For those of you particularly interested in this field, I can show you later the video footage of experiments on Shellie using military interrogation techniques. We produced some spectacular red lines that week!" Shellie's smile momentarily tightened into a grimace.

Chad glanced at his watch. "We have time for a few questions before lunch." Fifty-three hands rose into the air and undulated like a nest of angry snakes. "Yes, you with the green tie."

"How many other subjects besides Shellie have been tested with the WellMate?"

"There are five hundred volunteers in the core trial group who have been using WellMate for six months, with superlative results. I have also tested WellMate on another five hundred patients with pre-existing conditions. WellMate concurred with their doctors' diagnoses in 98.6% of cases. The discrepancy in the remaining 1.4% was proven to be due to doctor error. In the early stages of development, WellMate was tested extensively on animals. Consequently we foresee it also having significant applications in veterinary science. Due to the problematic nature of the experiments, however, Shellie is the only human subject in whom I have induced ill health in order to alter the readings. Next question."

"So far you've said that Shellie has been starved, sleep deprived and psychologically tortured. What else have you done to her?"

Chad gave a dry chuckle. "What *haven't* I done to her?" he said. He began to count off points on his fingers. "I've subjected her to extremes of heat and cold, exposed her to various viruses and bacteria, overfed her, underfed her, poisoned her, made her sit through forty eight hours of back-to-back horror movies, told her that her parents had died horribly in a house fire… of course, I'm always careful not to cause any damage that couldn't be undone. I doubt I would be attracting many investors if I had trotted Shellie out on stage in the state she was in after some of those experiments. Next question – the redhead down the back."

"This question's for Shellie. How much have you been paid to go through all this?" Shellie opened her mouth to answer the question, but Chad interrupted. "Oh, didn't I mention it before? Shellie is my wife. She did it all for love." At this, Shellie gave up all attempts to maintain her smile. She shook her head and glared at Chad as he focussed on his audience.

"You mentioned that the WellMate also measures emotional health," said a middle-aged man in the front row. Do we get to see a demonstration of this?"

Chad slapped his right palm to his forehead theatrically. "I'm sorry," he said, "I can be a bit of an absent-minded professor at times. I often overlook the emotional component of health. It's not my area of expertise."

"No kidding," muttered Shellie, too low for anyone to hear.

"There's nothing mysterious about emotions. They can be measured by changes in biochemistry, as this next screen will show."

The graphs displayed on the wall screen differed markedly from the previous ones. Almost all of them edged into the red. One in particular extended to its limit in the red zone, as if Shellie's emotional lifeblood had poured out onto the screen. A murmur ran through the audience. Chad looked at Shellie, his features creased in bewilderment.

"I tried to tell you," she said. She began peeling wires away from her body. The graphics on the screen wavered, and then flickered out entirely to leave the screen blank.

"Dr Goldsmith?" ventured a young woman in the middle of the room. "I didn't get a chance to read it all. What did that solid red line represent?"

Chad gave his answer to his wife's retreating back as she walked out of the room.

"It seems that she has run out of love."

Tracie McBride

Tracie McBride is a New Zealander who lives in Melbourne, Australia with her husband and three children. Her work has appeared or is forthcoming in over 80 print and electronic publications, including *Bleed, FISH* and the Stoker Award-nominated anthologies *Horror for Good* and *Horror Library Volume 5*. This collection contains much of the work that earned her a Sir Julius Vogel Award. She helps to wrangle slush for Dark Moon Digest and was the vice president of Dark Continents Publishing (2010 – 2014). Visitors to her blog are welcome at http://traciemcbridewriter.wordpress.com/.

* * *

Molly Rodman is currently a graphic designer and illustrator working in Los Angeles. As a recent graduate of the Rhode Island School of Design she has worked on packaging, concept design, visual effects, and illustration for companies including Hasbro, The Story Hat, Comfy Chair Games, and Prime Focus VFX. You can view more of her artwork on her website: www.pixieringillustration.com

Ghosts Can Bleed
ISBN: 978-4-82419-736-8

Published by
Next Chapter
2-5-6 SANNO
SANNO BRIDGE
143-0023 Ota-Ku, Tokyo
+818035793528
5th September 2024

Milton Keynes UK
Ingram Content Group UK Ltd.
UKHW041204051024
449185UK00005B/35